The Mistletoe Bet

MAREN MOORE

MAREN MOORE

(

Cover Design: Cat with TRC DESIGNS

Formatting: Maren Moore

FOR ALL MY HO HO HO'S WHO MADE THE NAUGHTY
LIST AND WISHED THAT HALLMARK MOVIES CAME WITH SPICE.

Xo, Santa

MAREN MOORE

Playlist

PARKER'S FAVORITES... NOT QUINN'S.

Mistletoe- Justin Bieber

Santa Baby- Kylie Minogue

Merry Christmas- Taylor Swift

All I Want for Christmas Is You- Mariah Carey

It's Beginning to Look a Lot like Christmas- Michael Buble

Have Yourself A Merry Little Christmas- Sam Smith

Baby, It's Cold Outside- Dean Martin

Blue Christmas- Elvis Presley

I'll Be Home- Meghan Trainor

White Christmas- George Ezra

Take Me Home For Christmas- Dan + Shay

MAREN MOORE

MAREN MOORE

Chapter One
QUINN

"HO-FREAKING-HO.....MERRY MY ASS."
- QUINN SCOTT

MAREN MOORE

4

❝Quinn, that dress is so lovely on you. It really accentuates your curves. You know, you are such a beautiful girl, and if you only lost a few…" Aunt Polly leans in and whispers, not so quietly, on the other side of her hand, *"pounds*, you would be so breathtaking."

'Tis the damn season.

"Thanks, Aunt Polly, I'm just going to um…get another drink. It was really nice talking to you and catching up. I hope you enjoy the party!" I hold up the almost empty glass flute and offer the best smile I can manage after being insulted directly to my face with her backhanded 'compliment.'

I thought the bright red, festive AF, empire-waist dress made of vintage satin did wonders for my body, but, as always, I'm only the 'pretty' fat girl. The 'you have such a lovely face,' but 'you would be so much prettier if only you were a little thinner' girl. Bringing the glass of champagne to my red-stained lips that match my dress, I down the last of the fizzling liquid and place the empty glass onto a waiter's tray as he passes by me.

While I sometimes miss home, the sleepy, snowy small town that I grew up in, the moment I return, I remember exactly what it was that made me leave Strawberry Hollow in the first place. The small-town gossip, everyone knows everyone kind of town.

Instead of subjecting myself to another 'kind' assault from my family, I grab my faux fur coat, slide it on then head straight for another glass of champagne. The table near the back door is full of glasses, so I swipe two with one hand, giggling to myself when the glass clinks together loudly, and tiptoe toward the patio and make my escape.

Fresh air and copious amounts of champagne are the only way I'm going to make it through this godforsaken Christmas party. The only way I'm going to survive being stuck with my family for the next week and all of their bothersome Christmas festivities is to drink whatever and whenever it's available.

I hate the holidays.

Actually, I *loathe* them.

Like more than anything.

Call me a Scrooge. The Grinch. The girl who hates Christmas.

The fact that I'm even at this stupid party to begin with is only due to the fact that my mother majorly guilt-tripped me into coming home for Christmas this year.

I was perfectly fine hunkering down for another New York winter, watching reruns of Gilmore Girls, and avoiding my family, phone, and email at all costs. The perfect vacation from work. One that I so desperately needed.

But instead, here I am. Enduring an entire seven days with my parents and brother because my mother is on a crusade to bring us all back together for the holidays. Oh, what fun it is...*not.*

Ho-freaking-Ho. Merry my ass.

Thankfully, my Apple Watch shows that it's after eight, which means I can potentially sneak away soon, in a few hours, if I'm lucky. Hopefully, the copious amount of champagne I've consumed so far will make the next hour or two a tad more bearable.

I push open the French doors, letting them fall shut

behind me, and step out onto the patio. It's lightly snowing, and cold as a witch's tit out here. But I'm alone, and the silence is a welcome reprieve after the last hour of small talk with extended family members that I can barely remember.

Shaking my head, I set the glasses down on the table. The outdoor dining table and sectional are surrounded by overhead heaters, as well as a massive fire pit in the middle, but that does nothing to stop the bitter cold from creeping in through my coat. Goosebumps erupt on my skin, and I rub my hands together to try and fight off the chill.

It's better than in there, I tell myself.

"Why are you standing out in the freezing cold...in *that*?" From behind me, a deep, gravelly voice interrupts my solitude.

He drags the last word out, laced with arrogance and bravado.

Without turning around, I know exactly who that voice belongs to. The same voice that sends a different kind of shiver down my spine, one that has *absolutely nothing* to do with the cold.

Parker Grant.

Charming playboy, handsome doctor, and the most sought-after bachelor in our hometown.

And...my brother Owen's best friend.

The same guy I've had a crush on since I was a preteen, when he was a gangly, tall teenager only a few years older than me. The guy I doodled in all of my notebooks, my first name with his last, covered in hearts. The first real crush I ever had, and the first one to subsequently break my heart, without him ever knowing.

Years later, and even now, all he has to do is speak and my thighs clench together in unrequited anticipation.

Not that I am still pining away for him. I let go of that silly teenage crush long ago. When I realized that I would never be the kind of girl he was looking for. I was simply his best friend's kid sister who tagged along and annoyed them, any chance I got.

I glance back over my shoulder and see Parker leaning against the pillar in a black sports coat and a tie covered in candy canes around his neck. So sinfully delicious, even with that ridiculous tie that I allow myself a few short seconds to drink him in before I turn back toward the dark tree line and take another hefty sip of champagne, draining half the glass.

"This dress is vintage Valentino, thank you very much."

He laughs, rough and low, and I swallow thickly, feeling it settle in the pit of my stomach.

"The party's inside, and here you are out here...all alone." He comes to stand next to me, resting his thick forearms on the balcony's railing. When he looks over at me, his dark, unruly hair falls across his forehead, and I immediately want to reach out and brush it away. "What's not to enjoy, Quinny?"

The use of my childhood nickname has me squinting my face in disgust. Typical Parker. We used to bicker constantly, he and Owen taking any opportunity they had to tease me.

"Can you not call me that? We're not kids anymore, Parker."

I sway slightly when the wind picks up. His hand darts out to steady me, sliding into my coat as he grips my hip tightly. The warmth of his fingers seep through my dress, and I clear my throat, grabbing onto the rail to ground myself.

"Trust me, I know." The deep, seductive tone catches me by surprise, and I find myself leaning slightly into his touch. His eyes drag down my body slowly, then flit back up to mine.

His eyes burn with intensity. The deep brown of his irises seemingly black in the darkness.

What's happening right now?

I've clearly had too many glasses of champagne.

Is...Parker...flirting with *me*?

No, of course not. *Quinn, no more champagne for you.* Actually, no, maybe I need *more* champagne because I'm clearly losing my mind.

I snap out of it, remembering his question. I tuck my long, dark hair behind my ear and avert my gaze. "I'm out here because I hate the holidays and I hate being home even more. My idea of a good time is not being stuck in a room full of people I barely remember and rarely ever see."

Parker frowns, revealing a shallow line between his dark brows as he does. "You used to love Christmas. You were obsessed with ice skating, decorating the tree. What happened?"

I grew up and realized that life changes in the blink of an eye. That's what happened. Once my parents divorced and my father moved out, everything changed. My parents hated to be around each other, so that was the end of us all being together.

Our holidays were split. Birthdays. Weekends.

I couldn't wait to leave this town behind, so the second I could, I fled to New York to pursue my career.

I didn't have time to enjoy things like holidays, especially not with my father, who I hardly knew anymore. Not when my only focus has been to advance in my career and make a name for myself.

I shrug, swirling around the remaining champagne at the bottom of my glass. "Life, I guess. I've got exactly zero Christmas spirit, and I'm counting down the seconds until I can board a plane back to what I now call home."

"It's been a while since you've been back home. I mean to Strawberry Hollow at least." His tone is cool and carries a hint of an unasked question.

Exactly four years. But who's counting?

"It has. My mom is on a mission to bring us all back together for the holidays. And you know Stacy…when she gets something in her head, it's happening." I sigh.

Parker laughs, nodding his head in agreement. "Yeah, your mom is definitely tenacious like that. I think it's mostly that she's trying to keep herself busy. Did you know she and the other ladies at the church have put together a caroling group?"

I didn't know that, but in truth, I'm not very close to my mother anymore. When we do talk, our conversations are short and to the point. The fact that Parker knows more about what she's doing than I do…suddenly makes me sad, even if I am part of the reason for the distance between us.

"Sounds like her." I drag my gaze to his and see that he's watching me intently. "What about you? How are things with you?"

The corners of his lips tug up and he shrugs. "Opened my own practice in town, still having dinner with my parents on Sundays. Working on the farm when they need me. Not much has changed since you've left, I guess."

That's partially true. The town has remained mostly the same: small, idyllic, almost untouched by the modernness of the outside world, it seems. But some things *have* changed. Parker, for example.

He's so much taller than I remember. His shoulders fill his jacket in a way that they wouldn't have four years ago, that much I know. It seems like in the time I've been gone, he's turned into a man that I no longer know.

"I always knew that you'd end up opening your own practice. When we were kids, you always took such care cleaning my scrapes and putting band aids on me when I'd fall while riding my bike or scratch myself up, trying to climb into the tree house following you and Owen." I laugh, shaking my head at the memory. Parker Grant spent a lot of time in our house growing up, so most of my memories as a kid include him.

My eyes drift back over his profile as he stares out into the darkness. His nose is slightly crooked from a fight when he was teenager, but if anything, it only makes him even more handsome. A dark brush of stubble is scattered along his jaw, and slightly down his neck. Rugged, yet refined.

Suddenly, he looks over, and I realize I've been caught admiring him.

I'm blaming it on the champagne and not the long-buried crush that's suddenly resurfacing.

"Christmas is magical, Quinn. I know you're a hotshot marketing executive now for a big Fortune 500, but maybe coming home is exactly what you needed, since you've seem to have forgotten that."

Scoffing, I reach for the champagne flute and carefully

bring it to my lips for a sip, the bubbles sliding down my throat with ease.

"This *champagne* is magic, Parker. But Christmas? Not so much. I don't know how I'm going to endure the next seven days being stuck at home. Mom is convinced that all we need is quality time together, and that she and Dad are capable of being in the same room without anything being thrown, but I'm calling bullshit. Christmas isn't magic; it's an excuse for people to get presents. Nothing more, nothing less. At least Owen has Cary to act as a buffer."

My brother and his fiancé, Cary, are high school sweethearts, and it's part of the reason he stayed behind in Strawberry Hollow. Now, he has a reason to be absent. Not me. I'm going to be stuck at my parents' beck and call.

"Eh, a week is nothing." His shoulder dips in a shrug. "Maybe you'll find out just how much you miss home now that you're back."

That, I sincerely doubt.

A strong gust of wind disrupts our quiet, seeping through my jacket and causing me to shiver violently. If I stay out here any longer, I'm going to freeze to death.

Clearly, Parker was right to ask why I was standing out in the cold in this dress and my fashionable, but hardly functional coat. As beautiful as it is, it is not meant for a snowstorm.

I quickly drink the remainder of the champagne in one swallow then set it down on the table. "Thanks for the company. I guess I better head back inside before Mom realizes I'm missing and sends out a search party."

"It was good catching up, Quinny," Parker says, a wistful look in his eyes.

"Yeah, it was," I say softly, our gazes locked. For a moment, neither of us say anything. A moment that suddenly feels intense and overwhelming, and honestly, a little confusing.

These old feelings resurfacing have taken me by surprise. I didn't expect to see him and feel anything but nostalgia.

Somehow, I tear my eyes away, then turn on my heels and walk back through the French doors toward the party. I feel his gaze on me until I slip back inside. The welcomed toasty air greets me, and I sigh, letting it thaw me.

I glance around the room until I spot Owen and Cary cuddled up in the corner, probably whispering sweet nothings in each other's ears. They're so in love, it's sick.

As happy as I am for my brother, I'm also a tad bit...

envious?

My love life consists of sporadic Tinder hookups, and that one guy from my building that keeps texting me "you up?" in the middle of the night.

Definitely no fairy-tale romance. Not that I'm looking for Prince Charming.

My job is my life.

My entire world revolves around One Click Marketing. Trying to make a name for yourself and working your way up the corporate ladder in a male-controlled industry is not easy. It just so happens that my boss is a grade-A misogynistic asshole, who gets off on making women feel inferior. If I hadn't spent the last almost five years of my life building my credibility, I would quit in a heartbeat. But, I'm not giving him the satisfaction of driving yet another woman out.

"Quinn?"

Mom's voice breaks through my thoughts. She's standing in front of me with a glass of creamy liquid, and my mood immediately perks up.

Grandma Scott's famous eggnog.

The one and *only* good thing about Christmas.

"Sorry, I was thinking about work." I plaster on a wide

smile, taking the glass from her extended hand. Just what I need to finish out the night.

Hopefully, unscathed, aside from a few fat jabs from Aunt Polly.

Mom's face softens, her eyes wrinkling slightly at the corners. "Quinn, you work too much. See, this is exactly why I wanted you home for Christmas with us. I want all of us together in the same place, enjoying the holiday and not worrying about work or anything else. I just miss you, honey. It's been four years since you've been home." Sadness drips from her tone, matching the expression in her eyes.

I hate when we have these conversations because I feel so immensely guilty. Even though the tension between her and Dad is part of the reason I stopped visiting for the holidays, it still hurts that things between us have gotten so distant. That my need for space continues to hurt her.

"I know, Mom. That's why I'm here. All yours for a whole week. I'm even participating in this Christmas musical, even though I would rather throw myself off the Empire State Building.."

The thought of this damn musical has the champagne ready to come back up.

She perks up, pulling me to her and smashing me against her chest. "I promise, my darling, it's going to be the best vacation ever. Even the musical! I'll make sure of it. Oh, by the way." Pulling back, she smirks and glances to the side.

"See that guy over there? Tall. Blond hair and chiseled jaw?"

I groan, unable to stop it from escaping my lips. "Did you seriously just say *chiseled jaw*? Have you been reading those smutty romance books again?"

"Quinn, hush." The peaks of her cheeks redden with a flush, and I smirk. "It's true, just look at him. He's the definition of chiseled. That's my new neighbor Amelia's grandson, Brent. Isn't he handsome?"

"Oh, no. No, no, no, absolutely not. Mom, you are not setting me up with anyone, ever. Especially not your neighbor's grandson!"

Mom rolls her eyes. "Well, you should at least think about it. You could invite him to dinner tomorrow. Owen invited Parker, and your dad will be coming with his new wife."

Surprisingly, I don't hear the usual thinly-veiled disgust in her mention of my father.

But that means that I don't even get a few days of preparation before we're all thrown together and expected to play nice. My dad's wife is only ten years older than me, and needless to say, I think she probably has more in common with me than with him. Not that I really know anything about her. I only met her once, the night of their wedding.

Following my mom's line of sight, I see the man she's talking about standing across the room with Amelia on his arm. She's not wrong...he is handsome, but regardless, I'm not interested.

I'm here for a week, and my life is not some cliché Hallmark movie, where the corporate girl falls for the sweet, small-town guy when she comes home for Christmas to save the family business or some other contrived festive nonsense.

Nope. Absolutely not happening.

The sooner the holidays can be over and I'm on a plane back to New York, the better.

"I'm just saying, Quinn. You spend too much time working. How will you ever settle down and have a family, if you're always working?" Mom reaches out to affectionately swipe her thumb along my cheek.

"Something tells me that I'll figure it out, Mom. If that's even what I decide I want. But I don't want you or Amelia matchmaking for me, okay? Please."

Finally, she sighs, nodding. "Fine. But dinner is still on. Sorry, sweets."

"Fantastic."

I take a hefty swig of the eggnog and play the part of dutiful daughter, making my way around the room and saying hello to our guests. Before I know it, the crowd has started to disperse, and not a moment too soon since my feet are aching from my new, unbroken-in Louboutins. I walk out of the dining room and into the kitchen, using the doorway to lean on as I pop the heel from my foot.

"Ugh," I moan the moment I can wiggle my freshly-painted toes freely, even though they ache with the movement.

Thank God the party is pretty much over. I'm all 'people'd' out for the night. Actually, for the rest of the year. I'll try again next year.

"I think you lost five inches from those heels."

When I look up, I see Parker has snuck up on me yet again, his hands shoved in the pockets of his slacks, a wry grin on his lips.

"Yeah, well, I was about to lose a toe if I kept those things on any longer," I mutter, sliding the other heel off. "I should've known not to wear heels that haven't been broken in, but I couldn't resist. Did you enjoy the party?"

Parker nods and reaches up, loosening the bright red tie around his neck so that it hangs open. "I did. I love a good party, especially when it's Christmas..."

Only then do I notice the Santa hat shaped cufflinks on his shirt, and I shake my head. "I swear, you are the most Christmas cheer person I've ever met. I don't know how you do it. Thinking about the next week is enough to make my stomach hurt, let alone be *excited*."

"That's because you're obviously the female equivalent of Scrooge, Quinny."

My eyes roll at his teasing, but then I notice what's above us.

Parker notices I'm staring up and his eyes drift to the green leafy plant with red berries directly over our heads.

Wonderful. Could this be any more cliché? In fact, it might possibly be *THE* Hallmark Christmas movie cliché. Just my luck.

"Mistletoe." He grins, stepping closer to me. "You know what this means?"

My heart begins to pound wildly. Surely, he doesn't mean...

He takes another step closer, and I swallow. My fingers tighten their grip around the heel of my shoe while the corners of Parker's lips rise into a full-blown smile that suddenly has my knees feeling weak.

"Sorry, Little Scott, but being the only person around here with real Christmas spirit, you know how important it is to me to follow the holiday traditions. And the mistletoe?" He points above us. "It's one of the most important ones."

I can't kiss Parker. He's...he's Owen's best friend. Not to mention, extremely dangerous for my heart. I can't chance resurrecting those old childhood crush feelings.

"I-"

Before I can even respond, he pulls me to him, sealing his lips over mine and silencing my protest.

Parker Grant is kissing me.

Parker Grant is kissing me!

It takes a second for my brain to catch up to what is actually happening. I think back to all the times that I dreamed of this very moment as a teenager, fantasized about him walking into my room, pulling me into his arms and kissing me until I was breathless.

His lips are firm and demanding, yet soft in a way that is completely unexpected. His hands slide into my hair, pulling me closer against him as his tongue teases the seam of my lips.

Lost in the moment, my heels clatter to the floor, breaking the spell between us.

Parker tears his mouth away and takes a step back.

Stunned, I reach up to touch my swollen and thoroughly kissed lips. I can't believe that just happened.

"You know what, Quinn?" Parker says, closing the space he just put between us. "I bet you, right here, right now, that if you give me these seven days you're home, I can make you fall in love with Christmas all over again."

His words take me back to when we were kids, when everything between us was an adventure, full of fun and games that we loved to play and never got old.

"Really Parker?" I say incredulously.

His shoulder rises in a shrug. "I know you, Quinn Scott, and I know that somewhere in there is the girl that used to wake up with me in the middle of the night, just to see if we could catch Santa. I know that your old Christmas spirit is there, and if you give me a week, just the seven days that you're home, I can make you love those things all over again. Love being *home* again. And if I can't, then I'll take your spot in the Christmas musical your mom has told the entire town you're performing in."

What? Christ on a cracker.

"Hmm. What's the catch?"

Parker shakes his head. "There isn't one. You can hand over the elf costume. Tights and all. That is...if I lose."

Now *this*...is a bet that I'm willing to take. God, not having to dress up in that stupid costume and prance around a stage? I'd do anything.

Well, practically *anything*. Desperate times call for desperate measures, and this is, for sure, a desperate measure.

Or... is it? Maybe I'm only saying yes because I want to climb Parker like a tree and deal with the consequences later, but either way...

"Deal. Because I know there is absolutely no way that I will ever love this stupid holiday again or love being home....so, you're on. Anything not to put on that stupid costume and be in that horrible play. I'm pretty sure Derick Michaels has worn it four years in a row, and I doubt it's been washed since."

Now this will be entertaining, because there's no possible way I can lose. The odds are fully-stacked against Parker, and I can't wait to revel in my win when I see him on that stage.

"What about you? What if you win, what do you get?" I ask, crossing my arms over my chest.

"If I win, then you're putting on the costume, and that's enough for me, Little Scott."

He grins and adds, "And no cheating. Anything's fair game and you have to give it a *real* shot. I know when you're bullshitting, so no funny business."

"Deal."

"A week from now, we'll meet under the mistletoe at your dad's annual Christmas party, and then we'll see."

There's absolutely no way that Parker Grant and his ridiculous Christmas cheer will be rubbing off or on me. Ever. Which means that I can kiss the ridiculous elf costume and that stupid play goodbye.

Thank God.

"Game on, Dr. Grant."

Grandma Scott's Famous Eggnog

Ingredients
6 LARGE EGG YOLKS
1/2 CUP GRANULATED SUGAR
1 CUP HEAVY WHIPPING CREAM
2 CUPS MILK
1/2 TEASPOON GROUND NUTMEG
PINCH OF SALT
1/4 TEASPOON VANILLA EXTRACT
GROUND CINNAMON , FOR TOPPING
ALCOHOL OPTIONAL— SEE NOTE

Directions

WHISK THE EGG YOLKS AND SUGAR TOGETHER IN A MEDIUM BOWL UNTIL LIGHT AND CREAMY.

IN A SAUCEPAN OVER MEDIUM-HIGH HEAT, COMBINE THE CREAM, MILK, NUTMEG AND SALT. STIR OFTEN UNTIL MIXTURE REACHES A BARE SIMMER.

ADD A BIG SPOONFUL OF THE HOT MILK TO THE EGG MIXTURE, WHISKING VIGOROUSLY. REPEAT, ADDING A BIG SPOONFUL AT A TIME, TO TEMPER THE EGGS.

ONCE MOST OF THE HOT MILK HAS BEEN ADDED TO THE EGGS, POUR THE MIXTURE BACK INTO THE SAUCEPAN ON THE STOVE.

WHISK CONSTANTLY FOR JUST A FEW MINUTES, UNTIL THE MIXTURE IS JUST SLIGHTLY THICKENED (OR UNTIL IT REACHES ABOUT 160 DEGREES F ON A

THERMOMETER). IT WILL THICKEN MORE AS IT COOLS.

REMOVE FROM HEAT AND STIR IN THE VANILLA, AND ALCOHOL*, IF USING.

POUR THE EGGNOG THROUGH A FINE MESH STRAINER INTO A PITCHER OR OTHER CONTAINER AND COVER WITH PLASTIC WRAP.

REFRIGERATE UNTIL CHILLED. IT WILL THICKEN AS IT COOLS. IF YOU WANT A THINNER, COMPLETELY SMOOTH CONSISTENCY, YOU CAN ADD THE ENTIRE MIXTURE TO A BLENDER WITH 1 OR 2 TABLESPOONS OF MILK AND BLEND UNTIL SMOOTH.

SERVE WITH A SPRINKLE OF CINNAMON OR NUTMEG, AND FRESH WHIPPED CREAM, IF DESIRED.

STORE HOMEMADE EGGNOG IN THE FRIDGE FOR UP TO ONE WEEK.

ALCOHOL OPTIONAL, SEE NOTE

ALCOHOL: IF YOU WANT TO ADD ALCOHOL TO YOUR EGGNOG, START WITH 1/4 CUP BRANDY, BOURBON, RUM OR WHISKY ADDED AT THE SAME TIME AS THE VANILLA, OR AFTER COOLING THE EGGNOG. ADD MORE TO TASTE, IF DESIRED.

YIELD: ABOUT 4 CUPS

Chapter Two
QUINN

"'TIS THE DAMN SEASON."
— QUINN SCOTT

MAREN MOORE

"Rise and shine, Quinn," my mother sing-songs from somewhere in the guest room I'm currently sleeping in. Well, trying to sleep in. Seconds later, blinding sunlight streams into the room, bathing me in warmth as she wrenches the curtains open. All. The. Way.

"Go away." I groan. I haul the blanket farther over my head, shielding myself from the light. "I am never leaving this bed. *Ever.*"

My entire body hurts; it feels like I got run over by a truck, and even Stacy's quest for family bonding isn't going to get me out of this bed. I'm faintly aware of Santa Claus is Coming to Town playing in the background, and the smell of fresh gingerbread.

I've woken up in hell. That's what's going on.

"I will not. It's nine a.m., and it is the most beautiful day outside. Plus, you have a visitor."

That gets my attention. I sit up abruptly, peering at her with one eye open.

"Visitor?"

Mom nods, a sly smile on her lips. She crosses her arms over her chest and peers down at me. "Dr. Parker Grant is here."

Dr. Grant.

My mother is referring to Parker as Dr. Grant. The man is practically her son. It's entirely too early for her theatrics.

"Okay...and? I'm sure he's here to do man shit with Owen."

"Nope, he's here to see *you.*"

Bringing my fingers to my forehead, I rub the tender, achy skin. Exactly how much champagne and eggnog did I have last night?

Oh my god. Shit. Shit. Shit.

The night comes flooding back in one tidal wave of bad decisions. Parker's lips on mine, his flirting...The *stupid* bet.

Great, Quinn, what in the hell have you gotten yourself into?

This was supposed to be a simple trip home, with the

goal of getting out of here as soon as I could and doing the least amount of holiday cheer possible. That plan definitely does not include engaging in silly Christmas bets with my off-limits brother's best friend.

"Hm. Interesting," Mom quips, turning back toward the doorway. Before she reaches it, she turns back and smiles over her shoulder. "Better fix that hair before you come downstairs."

With that, she walks out the door, humming. Almost as if she likes to see me tortured and hungover in pain.

I glance at my reflection in the vanity mirror next to my bed and groan again when I see my hair. It's standing in fifteen different directions, and it looks like there might *actually* be two turtle doves nesting in it.

Flopping back against the mattress, I flip onto my stomach, then grab the pillow and scream in true dramatic fashion. Day two in Strawberry Hollow and I'm already questioning my sanity for returning in the first place.

After taking the fastest shower known to man, brushing my teeth, quickly taming my hair and applying a small amount of makeup, I throw on clothes and walk downstairs. I'm greeted by so many Christmas decorations on every single surface of my childhood home, I want to vomit.

Tinsel, lights, Santas… the size of small toddlers. The Christmas tree itself is a whopping ten-foot tall Fraser fir that I'm pretty sure my mom loves more than both of her children combined. I've caught her staring at it several times since I got home, affection glowing in her eyes.

Gag me.

It's all too much. Honestly, Christmas is just one stressful day a year, where people come together to give each other gifts. I don't get the hype.

"Good morning."

Parker's, entirely too cheery for this early in the morning, voice comes from the kitchen. I turn to find him sitting at the bar, a mug in front of him featuring a flurry of gnome elves on the outside with piping hot coffee inside.

I can smell its sweet aroma from here, and my mouth immediately begins to water.

Coffee is the only thing I can truly think about right now.

Well, that, and the fact that Parker looks entirely too handsome and he just happens to be sitting in my kitchen.

He's wearing a dark green Henley, the cotton fabric

hugging the sculpted muscles of his forearms and biceps, with a pair of worn jeans that fit his thick thighs perfectly and a pair of work boots.

How is a doctor this fit? Honestly. It's ridiculous.

"No little children to save this morning, Doctor?" I grumble as I pass by him, making a beeline for the coffee maker.

"Took the morning off. I'll head in this afternoon. You know, Quinny, you've always been a true ray of sunshine in the mornings, but today, you are really something," he says.

I narrow my eyes at him before turning to grab, you guessed it, a Christmas mug from mom's cabinet. They are all Christmas mugs.

Every. Single. One.

There's one that says *Mayberry Inn* from Hollyridge, my mom's favorite vacation locale. A snowman with an elf. Santa and his reindeer. *A Christmas Story* mug. Jesus, there's even a goat riding a sleigh.

It's not as if I had a non-cheerful choice to choose from.

At least this one is extra-large, even if it is in the shape of an elf's shoe. Bells and all. They jingle when I carry it over to the coffee pot.

When I lift my gaze, I see Parker smiling all too smugly. "This is going to be so much fucking fun."

Ignoring him, I grab the coffee pot and fill the cup to the brim, skipping sugar and creamer all together. Black coffee isn't for the weak. I breathe in the scent of the coffee and then take a large sip, savoring its bitter taste on my tongue. Of course, my mother is brewing peppermint mocha flavored coffee. Because why wouldn't she be during the holidays?

My God.

I'm too hungover for this. My head hurts all the way down to my toes. That was probably the Louboutins, but how can I be sure?

"Not sure I can brave the world today, my head hurts and the sunlight burns my eyes. Honestly, I'm sure you don't want me raining on your Christmas parade," I tell him, eyebrows raised.

At this point, I'm not above bribing him to get out of this bet that I drunkenly agreed to.

"Nope. Not happening. You are not getting out of this bet, Quinn Scott," he says as if he can read my mind. "If nothing, are you not a woman of your word?"

Low blow.

"Fine. But please for the love of God, nothing physical. I need at least thirty-six hours to recuperate. I'm not twenty-one anymore, Parker. Hangovers take at least two business days to go away. Old age does that to ya."

Nothing but the truth. Millennials will get it.

"You're not even thirty, Quinn," Parker retorts. "Quit complaining. C'mon, pour that in a thermos to go and grab two pain killers, I've got a whole morning planned."

"Look, I've only got six days to make you less grinchy and more festive. Sorry, but green tights aren't my thing. So, let's go. I can't waste a single minute, Santa himself knows I'm going to need every one of them." He tosses me a smirk, combined with a wink, then strides out of the kitchen, leaving me alone with my coffee.

Now I can't stop imagining Parker in those fitted green tights, and I can imagine how his di-

"Quinn!" he calls.

"Fine, fine, I'm coming. Jesus!"

After saying a quick goodbye to Mom, I walk outside and climb into Parker's truck, thankful that the snow has stopped and the sun is out, making it a little warmer outside. Today, though, I dressed for the occasion, not wanting to repeat my mistake from last night. Even though it *was* vintage Valentino, I almost froze my nipples off.

Parker's truck is older, and it smells just like him. The seats are worn and soft beneath my fingers. The smell of pine and old leather clings to the air, and I immediately sink back into the old bucket seat. He's had this same truck since I was in high school, and I'm a little surprised that he never upgraded. Since he's a fancy doctor and all. I feel like he should drive an Audi, or something. Not a beat up old truck that's older than he is.

"You look like you've seen a ghost of Christmas past," he says, sliding in beside me.

"You're getting too good at the festive puns. I just remember riding in the middle there," I smile wistfully as I point to the bucket seat, "all through high school. My head hit that roof more times than I can even count. I'm pretty sure I have a permanent bump."

His laughter reverberates inside the cab of the truck, making my stomach do a weird dip. I try to focus on buckling up, and not on the way the fabric of his shirt stretches across his wide shoulders as he reaches forward to put the truck in drive.

"Those were the days, huh? It feels like forever ago," he mutters.

It does, and I guess that's partially my fault, since I haven't been home in so long. Mostly in avoiding the situation with my parents, but also because I felt like this town had nothing to offer me. The only way I was ever going to make something of myself was to get out while I could. And I did. I went to school at NYU and interned at the firm I'm currently at while I was getting my degree.

"So, where are you kidnapping me to today?" I chirp, my grin widening when he cuts his eyes at me.

"You'll see when we get there."

Hm. "What about a clue?"

Parker shakes his head, then reaches toward his old dial radio and cranks up the volume, classic Christmas music filling the cab.

"You are *already* killing me."

"I told you, Quinny, I'm winning this bet. After this, I've gotta handle something at the office, but I'm going to pick you up later for part two of today's festivities."

"Sure." I turn toward him. "I promised Owen and Cary that I would help them pick out a gift for mom later, but I should be home right before dinner time. It's so weird having to drive everywhere again. Or well…have everyone drive me since I don't have a vehicle anymore.

I just take the subway and Uber everywhere I need to go back in New York."

Parker's eyes find mine and he nods. "You're a big-time city girl now. Probably weird to come back to a town this small again, even if it is home."

"Yeah." Tearing my gaze from him, I stare out the windshield as the familiar landscape of my childhood whips by, somehow everything looking the same yet different. There are the same places we frequented in high school like The Frost Top that serves the best ice cream in the world. Owen and Parker would take me every Friday, and it was the highlight of my entire week. There's also the same two stoplights, the high school that I graduated from, and the charming city hall, that's over a hundred years old, still stands proudly.

"Miss it?"

His voice breaks through my thoughts, and I snap my gaze to his. "Absolutely not. The best thing I ever did was get out of this town."

"If you say so, Quinny. Over there is my practice," Parker says, pointing to a small white building with light blue shutters and a matching door. It's adorable, and not at all what I was expecting. Just by looking at the exterior, I can tell how welcoming it is.

"You'll have to show me around before I leave."

"Don't worry, it's on the list."

My eyes widen, completely thrown off by what he just said. "Parker Grant, please tell me you don't have an actual list. Tell me you did not make a list to win this bet."

His shoulders shake and lift in a shrug, not bothering to hide his gruff laugh. "All's fair in The Mistletoe Bet. Besides, I'm a doctor, Little Scott. Of course I've got a list, and I'm checking it twice. I told you, I'm winning this damn bet. You'll see. Make fun of my list all you want after I win."

I have to see it.

"Let me see."

"Abso-fucking-lutely not. Hell no. Why would I give you access to my winning plan? Nah. Sit back and buckle up, baby. You're in for a ride."

Not sure if those words should excite or terrify me.

Half an hour later, Parker pulls the truck off the highway on the very outskirts of town, exiting down a dirt and gravel road with a huge sign that says *Kringlewood Christmas Tree Farm*.

"A tree farm?" I ask, my brows pulling together in

confusion.

"Yep. Figured I'd bring you along as I got mine. Nothing says Christmas like picking out a tree and decorating it."

Just the thought of physical labor today actually makes me sweat. After last night, I am not in any shape to do anything that requires exerting a lot of effort.

"Fantastic." Settling back against the seat, I turn my head toward the window and let my gaze fall on the treeline as Parker's truck bumps along down the dirt road.

I can feel his eyes on me more than once, but I never look his way, opting for silence until we arrive at the Tree farm, and he puts the truck in park.

"Quinn, it's not going to be that bad. I promise, I'll do all the heavy lifting. All you have to do is help me pick it out and stand there and look pretty," Parker teases, placing his hand on my thigh to get my attention.

And it does, but not in a way that benefits either of us.

One simple touch from Parker, and my body responds. As much as I wish it wasn't true, I can't deny the attraction I have to him, and have had since we were younger.

But that's all it is. Chemistry. Attraction.

Which is exactly why I've spent the entire morning *not*

thinking about the kiss we shared. Because it is not going to help the situation, whatsoever.

"If you say so, Dr. Grant."

He shakes his head at my dramatics and opens his door, sliding out of the cab of the truck. Before I can even get my door open, he's walking around the front and opening it for me.

"What a gentleman, thank you. So, since we're getting a tree, does that mean that you moved out of your parents' place or…"

I should probably have paid more attention when Owen talked about Parker, but honestly, the less I knew about home, the better. It was easier to acclimate to my new life in New York that way.

"I moved out about a year after I started my practice," he says, his chocolate eyes holding mine. "I've got a place up on the hill. Worked with the builder and architect for two years till it was built. In my spare time, I like to build things. Not that I've got much of it. But I just hired a new nurse practitioner at the office, and she's taking some of the load off of me. Hence, the time off this morning to come here," Parker says, reaching into the bed of his truck for a hacksaw and some rope. The two most important things we'll need, if we're leaving here with a tree.

He leads the way to the front entrance, and I drag my gaze over the farm in front of us. Now, I can see why Parker chose to come here. It's breathtaking.

There are acres and acres of land with hundreds of rows of trees, all differing in size and shape. The sun is high in the sky above us, causing the light layer of snow beneath our feet to melt, leaving behind shallow puddles of water.

The smell of pine and woodsy earth makes me think about all of the times that we came here as a family to pick out a tree. I'm surprised by just how much it makes me miss those days.

"Wow," I breathe, turning to face Parker, not letting myself get back in my head, "I'm glad you're finding a way to balance everything. Hotshot doctor and all." It's my turn to give him shit just like he's been giving me.

"Nah, the only hotshot here is you, Little Scott." Parker bumps my shoulder while we walk. "Becoming a doctor was kind of just the easy answer. I knew I wanted to be a doctor, to help people. My dad always told me growing up that if I did something that I loved, I wouldn't work a day in my life, and it's true. Sometimes I'm tired and sometimes it's a hard day, but I love what I do."

"I'm glad to hear that, Parker," I tell him as we walk.

His lips turn into a grin, "Thanks Quinny."

There are families all around us, children weaving in and out of the trees, chasing each other as they laugh in delight. Even though I'm completely anti-Christmas, it does make me smile. The joyful look on their faces is contagious.

I'm not a complete ice queen. Just a little Jack Frost-ish when it comes to the holidays and Christmas cheer.

"Parker Grant?" A voice sounds from behind us, and when I turn I see a man holding two little girls in each arm with blonde hair the same shade as his. Standing by his side is a dark haired woman with bright red lips and a kind smile.

The man's face is familiar, but it's been so long since I've been home, I can't place it.

Parker's face morphs into surprise as a wide smile settles on his lips, "Graham, how are you? How are my favorite girls?"

He walks over and tickles them both, causing them to giggle in delight. Both of his little girls are wearing matching outfits. Green turtleneck sweater onesies, and bright red wool leggings. They've got cute little beanies on their heads complete with pompoms. I can see why Parker is so smitten.

Oh God... seeing Parker interacting with these adorable little twins is not good for my heart.

My gaze drifts back to the man, and after a few seconds I realize who he is. He's the same age as my brother and Parker, and I think I met him once or twice back in high school. I think he plays professional hockey if I'm remembering correctly.

"They're getting bigger every day man. I can't believe how fast time has flown." Graham says, glancing down at his daughters with so much love that it makes my heart squeeze.

Parker nods, "That's what happens. You blink and time has flown by. Graham, Emery... this is Quinn Scott. She was a few years behind us in class. She's here visiting for the Holidays. She lives in New York City now."

They both smile and offer me a wave which I return.

"I was going to say, why haven't I met you yet? I moved from Chicago last year and am still trying to make friends. I'm an extrovert so I need all the human interaction." She says, and I laugh.

"I'm just in town visiting my parents, but we should totally get dinner before I leave?"

The smile on her face is genuine, and I immediately like this girl.

"Cool." She says.

"How are you, Emery?" Parker asks, directing his question to her.

The woman smiles, pushing her dark hair out of her eyes, "I'm good, thank you for asking. I need to schedule their one year checkup soon with your office."

"Absolutely. Call me on Monday and we can get it set up." Parker says to her then tickles the girls once more and claps Graham on the back. "Talked to Lane the other day. I heard something about a charity game happening again this year?"

"Yeah, you gonna join us?" Graham asks.

"Eh, maybe so. Let's get together soon and talk the logistics. I've gotta go find us a tree before she drags us out of here."

I narrow my eyes at him, and scowl. I didn't want *everyone* to know that I'm a Scrooge.

"Have fun! Here, take my number." Emery says.

After pulling my phone out, she quickly rattles off her

number and we all say goodbye.

Parker turns to face me, coming to a complete stop in front of a bunch of trees "Alright, Little Scott, which one are we taking home?"

That all look the same. Mostly.

"Well, that one over there *isn't* it."

He looks at the tree, then back at me. "Why not?"

I roll my eyes, gesturing toward the tree. "Er, well, first of all, it's not...*girthy* enough. You know, that really matters."

Parker laughs. "Okay, so we obviously want a tree that's really thick and girthy. Make sure it's full of fluff and the circumference is wide. Got it."

Jeez, who knew that talking about Christmas trees could be so...dirty?

"Yep, that sounds about right. And you don't want it to be too short and fat because then it just looks like a sausage."

"So not too short, not too tall." His eyes shine with amusement, and I can tell he's getting way too much enjoyment out of teasing me.

Prick.

I'm only here so I can win this stupid bet and get out of

this ridiculous play that my mother insists on forcing me to be in.

"Yes, exactly. I'm sure we'll find one that's the perfect size."

Turns out, it's not exactly easy to find the *perfect*-sized Christmas tree when we disagree on the actual size of it.

I like the tall, full trees, and Parker is more drawn to short, fat trees, and honestly, it's a travesty.

I groan when he, once again, leads me to a tree that's the size of an Oscar Meyer fricking Weiner and bring my hands to my hair exasperatedly. "Parker, what is really the problem here? Why do you like these short, fat trees? Didn't we agree that the bigger, the better? What about this one?"

I gesture to a tree that's at least two feet taller than Parker and full of girth like it should be. Not to mention it looks healthy. The needles are fresh and green and don't look dried out at all. It even has the perfect branch at the top for a topper.

The perfect Christmas tree and this man is currently staring at it like it's the ugliest thing he's ever seen.

"The problem is that you're picking out trees that won't even fit in my living room, Quinn. Fuck, that thing belongs in Rockefeller Center, not my house. Hell, are you gonna carry it back to the truck because I may have a decent set of muscles, but that thing is huge."

I shuffle on my feet, my hands on my hips, as we appear in a standoff over this damn tree. I shouldn't even notice how sexy he looks with the sleeves of his Henley pushed up, or the way the corded muscles in his forearms ripple as he waves the hacksaw around.

This moment brings me back to when we were kids. Everything was a debate between the two of us. No matter the topic. It's like we both loved to get some kind of reaction out of the other.

Obviously that's one thing that hasn't changed at all.

"You're impossible! This tree is the perfect height, and it will fit. We'll *make* it fit."

"You know what? Fine. If this is the tree you want, fine. But, if it doesn't fit, then that's your ass, Quinn Scott."

"Fine."

I cross my arms over my chest and level my stare. He drug me out here to pick out this stupid tree as part of our bet.

"You gonna stand there looking pretty or help me?" he mutters, dropping down beside the tree's stump.

My eyes widen. "Help you? What do you expect *me* to do? That tree is twice my height."

Parker looks like he might actually use that hacksaw to murder me at any moment, instead of cutting down the tree in question, and it makes me grin. I used to love to push his buttons anyway that I could, and it's nice to know that even after all these years, I've still got it.

"Christ Quinn. Just hold it steady for me, I'm going to saw the trunk and I need you to hold it up until I'm done. Can you do that?"

Can I? Sure. Do I really want to? Absolutely not. I thought we agreed on no physical activities with the way that my head has been pounding since I woke up this morning.

Do I really want to be here at all?

The answer is no.

But, I'm as competitive as I am determined, and that means that there is no way Parker Grant is winning this damn bet, come hell or high Christmas trees.

"Yes, I can *hold* the tree, Parker."

Marching over, I grab a branch and brace myself as he begins to saw at the stump. The entire tree shakes with the force of his movements, and after what feels like three hours have gone by, the tree starts to lean heavily toward me.

Shit, this thing is heavier than I anticipated.

While trying to hold it up, my hair gets tangled in one of the branches, and I yelp, accidentally letting it slide down, which obviously does not help the mess I've gotten myself in, and each time it slips down, it tugs harder at the hair wrapped around the branch.

"Shit. Fuck. Oh God. *PARKER!*" I yell. "Uh, I need a little help."

"Jesus Christ, Quinn, I've almost got it. Just hold it for another second," he calls from by my feet.

"I'm not going to last another second or I'm going to be bald. My hair, it's tangled."

I hear a string of curses, and then Parker is in front of me, red-faced, and breathing heavy. "What's wrong?"

I can't exactly move my head, since my hair is completely wrapped in the tree, so I just look up. "My hair is tangled in the tree branches."

Parker drags his gaze up, seeing the disaster of my hair, and sighs heavily before quickly getting to work. It takes a few minutes to get me untangled, and for the first time in my life, I'm cursing the fact that my hair is so damn long.

"Almost done."

"Sorry. You gave me one job and I failed at it." I squeak as he tugs a strand free from the branch.

I can feel his eyes on me when he pulls the last strand free. "It's all good. Now that we've gotten this larger-than-life tree you insisted on, how about we get it loaded up?"

The place where my hair was caught is sore now, my scalp sensitive to the touch, and I wince when my fingers brush against it.

Parker sees that and his brow furrows. "Shit, I'm sorry, Quinn, I didn't even check to see if you were okay. Here, let me see."

With one hand, he carefully sets the tree on the ground and gently pulls me to him, his strong fingers tangling in my hair as he inspects.

"There's no open cut or any blood that I can see. It'll probably just be sensitive for a couple of days. You can put an ice pack on it once you get home."

It's only my second day here and I've got the worst hangover in the history of the world, and my head hurts twice as bad as it did when I woke up this morning.

"Let's get you home, Little Scott. Give you time to rest for the festivities that I have planned for tonight.

Oh, goodie.

"Can't wait," I mutter, dropping my head into my hands.

Two days almost down, only five more to go.

Let's just hope the next week flies by with no more "incidents."

"What did you tell Owen when you asked him to drop you off?" Parker asks, shutting the heavy door of his rustic-style home behind me. I pause, taking it all in.

I'm not sure what I was expecting when he said that he built a house, but this was certainly not it. His house is a two-story, modern log cabin, for lack of a better way to explain. Everything seems to be made from wood, with hints of modern industrial throughout.

Although it's not what I expected, it fits Parker.

"I just told him I was helping you with something for your office. Marketing-related. I don't think he's capable of seeing anything but Cary. It's disgustingly cute." I laugh as I drag my finger along the raw wood of his foyer table. There are exposed knots inside the wood, and it looks as if Parker found it out in the forest and carried it directly in here, throwing a photo frame and a bowl for keys on top of it and calling it a table. "Your house is beautiful, Parker."

"Thank you, I've spent a lot of time on it. I knew exactly what I wanted, just had to bring it to life." He leans against the dark granite bar, the dark henley he's wearing pushed up at the sleeves, exposing his thick-corded forearms.

Since I arrived back home, I found myself noticing little things I hadn't paid much attention to before. Specifically, just how good Parker Grant looks wearing nothing but a worn pair of jeans and an old henley. And how ever since he kissed me last night, I can't stop thinking about how good he smells.

There are a lot of reasons why I shouldn't be thinking about that kiss; yet tonight, I can't seem to stop. The most important being the fact that Parker and I would never, and will never, be a thing. I live in New York, while he lives here.

I knew one thing for certain. I would never live in my hometown again. Never.

Not to mention, he's my brother's best friend, and he's practically a part of our family.

And all those factors are a recipe for disaster.

"I got two cartons of your grandma's eggnog, you want some? I figured with your aversion to all things Christmas, you could use a little something to get you by," Parker says, his pine-colored eyes sparkling with amusement. I'm glad he gets so much pleasure from teasing me.

Truly.

"Trying to get me drunk, Dr. Grant, so you have the advantage?"

I cross my arms over my chest and wait for his response. Though, I'm only teasing. I don't think there's an ungentlemanly bone in Parker's body, which is actually quite unfortunate because I can think of several scenarios where not being a gentleman is a good thing.

Stop it, Quinn. This is not helping.

"It's just fucking eggnog, Quinn." He laughs and shakes his head, his dark hair falling across his forehead as he does. He lifts his hand then runs his fingers through it to push it back from his face as he turns to the cabinet, grabbing two glasses from the shelf. When he turns back to face me and sets the glasses down on the granite, he looks up, waiting for my answer.

"Sure, but only because it would be rude to make you

drink alone."

"Yeah, okay."

His voice is dripping with sarcasm, and it makes me smirk. *Catching on quickly, Dr. Grant.*

He pours us each a hefty class of eggnog, then holds up his glass.

"To Christmas spirit."

I can't stop the eye roll that ensues, but still, I raise my glass and carefully clink it against his as I say, "To our competitive nature."

Parker's head shakes as he laughs, and only then, standing across from him, his kitchen island separating us, do I notice the small dimples in his cheeks that seem to pop when he smiles.

God, he's ridiculously handsome.

Not the awkward teenager I used to know. No, Parker is all man.

"You ready to decorate the tree?"

Bringing the eggnog back to my lips, I take a sip, savoring the sweet creamy taste on my tongue. "As ready as I'll ever be."

I follow behind Parker as he leads me into the living room.

"I'm going to let Marshmallow in really quick," he says, mentioning the golden retriever he's had since we were younger. He walks over to the back door and opens it, letting the dog run freely through the house.

He heads straight for me, jumping when he finally gets to me, almost knocking me over.

"Marshmallow! You spoiled rotten boy," I coo, petting his head, "I missed you so much."

He peppers my face with wet, slobbery kisses, showing he missed me too.

"Bed Marshmallow," Parker says, grabbing him by the collar and leading him to the ginormous fluffy bed by the recliner. He gives him a sweet pet, then turns to face me.

I drag my eyes over the room, noting the comfortable furniture spread around it. His couch and recliner are a deep brown leather that complements the rest of the house, and surprisingly, there's a large animal skin rug covering the floor in front of the fireplace.

My eyes widen in horror.

"What?" he asks, then follows my gaze to the large rug.

His laugh echoes off the walls of the living room, making my gaze snap to his. "It's faux fur, Quinn. Don't look so horrified."

"Okay. That's good. I was uh… questioning you there for a second. I love the fireplace. The details are incredible." Reaching out, I run my fingers along the smooth wood.

The mantle in front of us is raw, exposed wood that has been sanded, so it's smooth with a shiny clear coat. It's gorgeous.

"Thanks. I made that last summer."

His words make me pause. He made it? I knew he was into woodworking; I just didn't realize…

"Don't look so shocked, Quinny."

Parker's use of my nickname has me turning to face him. "Quinn. It's just Quinn." I glance back at the framed photo that sits on the mantle. It's a photo of Parker and his parents at his graduation. "How are your parents?"

"They're good. Mom spends most of the day working at the nursing home. She volunteers there a few days a week, sometimes on the weekends. It keeps her busy. When she's not volunteering, she's knitting. Be careful, if you see her out and about, she'll have a Christmas sweater on you faster than you can blink."

"Oh God," I groan, my eyes widening, "Tell me you're joking."

"*With* a matching scarf."

I shiver in horror. Nope. Absolutely not. There are a lot of things that I'll do for the people that I love, but I'm drawing the line at Christmas sweaters with matching scarves.

Shaking my head vehemently, I take another sip of eggnog, and then I think…there's a reason this eggnog is famous, and it's not just for its deliciousness. It's potent. The kind of drink that sneaks up on you.

My head is beginning to feel light and fuzzy, so I turn and set my now almost empty glass down on the coffee table.

"I forget how strong that stuff is. Better put me to work before I'm completely useless," I say.

Parker walks over to the clear tubs with red and green lids that are stacked neatly in the corner of his living room. I completely ignore the way the corded muscles of his forearms flex as he picks up a box and carries it over to the coffee table and sets it down with a huff. "My mom sent a few totes over, full of shit she wanted me to have. This is the first year I'm going to have a tree."

"Really? You're practically Buddy the Elf, and this is the first time you're putting up a tree?" I say incredulously. I'm shocked that he hasn't ever had a tree, not with how much he loves the holidays. It wouldn't surprise me if he had a Santa costume tucked away somewhere, just waiting to be worn.

Carefully unpacking the box of decorations, he shrugs. "Well, I work so much and spend the holidays at their house that I never prioritized getting a tree. I didn't get to participate in as many activities as I wanted to because of my schedule."

He hands me a box of multicolored Christmas lights.

"Which is why I'm looking so forward to dragging you along to all of them this year. It'll be fun, Quinny. Like a Christmas-version of torture." When his smile widens at my annoyance, I want to smack it right off of him, if only he wasn't so damn handsome.

"You're taking way too much joy in this. It's sadistic, Dr. Grant," I spout back.

"Nah, you not loving Christmas and being the Grinch, but less green...*that's* sadistic. It's my job to bring you back to the good side." He turns his back to me then and helps me string the lights along the branches, wrapping them around the tree as I stew in silence.

"Well, I'm here, aren't I?" I bump his shoulder teasingly.

Once the lights are on the tree, he stands back and admires our work. As much as I want to complain while being subjected to Christmas torture…something tells me that this is better than the alternative, and that's being stuck at home with my mother or being dragged around town for errands.

I can do this. If it gets me out of the house, out of my mother's reach and off that stage in a pair of green tights… it's worth it.

The bonus is spending time with Parker.

Together, we unpack all of the clear totes and set the boxes of ornaments and various decorations out, then begin to put them on the tree. Parker refills our cups, more than once, and halfway through decorating the tree, when he trips over an extra set of tangled lights, narrowly escaping falling in a heap on the floor, I double over laughing so hard that I almost fall to the floor myself.

All while Mariah Carey croons in the background, making the entire situation even funnier.

"Who knew Christmas lights could be a hazard," I choke out, still laughing. Tears still wetting my cheeks as I struggle to compose myself. "I'm sorry, I'll stop. I'll stop."

Dr. Christmas Cheer is not so cheery at me laughing

at him. He's standing next to the couch, his arms crossed over his chest, trying to hold back his own laugh.

Looking sexier than ever, which I shouldn't notice, but I do. It's not like I have any choice in the matter, not where Parker is concerned. He has this affect on me, whether I want to react or not.

He steps forward, towering over me, his eyes darkening as he does, and not for the first time tonight, I think…

I am so screwed when it comes to this man.

How to win The Mistletoe Bet
and make Quinn fall in love...

1. Go to tree farm. Everyone loves a tree farm.
Right...?

2. Decorate said tree. Lots of eggnog

3. Definetley have Marshmallow around.
He's too cute to dislike.

4. Iceskating? It was her favorite when we were kids

THE OFFICE OF
DR. PARKER GRANT

Chapter Three
QUINN

"GRANDMA SCOTT'S FAMOUS EGGNOG.
THE ONE AND *ONLY* GOOD THING ABOUT CHRISTMAS."
- QUINN SCOTT

"Has anyone ever told you that mouth of yours is going to get you in trouble, Quinn?" he whispers hoarsely, agonizingly low as he holds my chin between his fingers. His gaze is so intense, I feel it everywhere, in places that I shouldn't, despite the fact that it never leaves mine.

And I definitely should not be pressing my legs together in response to his touch, or the way his raspy voice seems to slither down my body and effortlessly take control of me.

Shit, get it together, Quinn.

Since when do you throw your morals and good sense out the window just because a man shows you attention?

Probably because it's been so long since a man has touched you at all, my vagina responds.

Marshmallow comes barreling off of his bed, knocking

me into Parker. My hands fly to his shirt, fisting in the soft fabric to keep myself upright.

"Oof," I mutter, the sudden intrusion taking me by surprise.

"Marshmallow!" Parker yells, dropping his hands from my chin and reaching his strong arms around my back to steady me. "That damn dog. Sorry, he's got so much spastic energy sometimes."

Parker takes a step back, his hands dropping from my back, and it does nothing to extinguish the heat coursing inside me.

I'm horny, and now the eggnog is making me brave.

What a combination.

"It's fine, seriously. I love sweet Marshmallow," I murmur, bending down to pet his soft golden retriever hair.

It's a good thing that Marshmallow interrupted when he did because lord knows what would have happened. What could have happened, that might have happened had we stood there even a second longer.

We continue to decorate the tree, Parker on his side and me on mine, a heavy tension hanging between us, but I push it away, opting to look through the last box of ornaments on the coffee table.

"Oh my god." I laugh as I pick up an ornament with a photo of the three of us on it. Me being squished between Owen and Parker. All of us are covered head to toe in snow, looking like wet puppies. "Do you remember this?"

Turning toward Parker, I hold up the square ornament to show him.

His expression softens, and he steps closer, lifting it from my hand.

"Jesus, I was a fucking nerd back then. Look at those glasses," he says, running his thumb along the old photograph.

"I mean, I think we all were doing our own thing back then. We were kids, trying to find our place in the world."

He nods. "I remember it like it was yesterday. You followed us around everywhere, like a little shadow. Wherever we went, there you were."

"Hey, I can't help it that you guys were the only choice for friends around here. "

I gingerly lift the ornament onto the tree, securing it to a branch in the middle and turn back to Parker. "I miss those memories sometimes. What's left?"

He glances down at the boxes and picks up the lone

item at the bottom of the last box. "Looks like just the angel. My mom gave me this one, passed down from Grandma Grant. I can't believe this thing is still in one piece, honestly. Here, let me go grab the ladder and we can put it on the tree."

"No, just give me a boost. I can put it up there faster than it takes you to go get the ladder and set it up," I tell him, taking the angel from his hands. "Unless you think I'm too heavy."

Sometimes I forget that I'm not a size zero.

Parker scoffs, then bends and scoops me up as if I weigh nothing, securing his arms under my ass, tightly looping his arms around my thighs. Without a word, he lifts me well past his chest. I try not to think about the fact that he's touching me, and instead, focus on the task at hand: getting this angel on the top of the tree and making sure it's straight.

"Okay, wait, a little closer," I say.

"How close? I can't see anything." Parker's muffled words come from behind me.

I guess I didn't realize how close his face is to my ass.

"Just a little. Okay, a little more to the right." I go to set the angel on the tree, but he steps a little too far to the right, causing me to wobble slightly. With nothing to grab onto, I flail in the air momentarily before, somehow, he rights us both, without me crashing to the ground.

"Quinn, I can't see anything between your ass and the sweater. Gotta give me some direction," he says.

Listen, I'm finding it very hard to concentrate, okay? *Sue me.*

"Um, okay, one step to the right. Now, just a little higher and that should do it."

I bet now he's cursing me even more for my choice in tree. The thought makes me giggle and I feel Parker grunt, then hoist me all of three centimeters higher.

Carefully, I slide the angel onto the lone branch at the top of the tree, and sigh, once it's safely there.

"Got it!"

Parker immediately lowers me, his hands sliding up my body as I glide down against every inch of him. Slowly, I turn to face him, a proud smile stuck on my lips.

"See? No ladder necessary," I breathe, glancing back up at my work. "What do you think?

Silence meets my question, so I look back at Parker and see that he's not looking at the tree at all.

He's looking at me.

I should back up, put space between us. Move to the other side of the room and forget that this stupid bet is even a thing.

But I don't.

Instead, I step closer. Against my better judgment. Because, really, who cares about judgment? I don't. Not right now. Not when I'm this close and surrounded by all that is Parker Grant.

"Quinn…" Parker's voice comes out hard, full of warning.

For him? Or for me?

I don't have the words to respond. Not ones that would make a difference. My head is swimming with eggnog, and something entirely different is coursing through my veins.

I want Parker, and I don't care about the consequences.

One way or another, I'm leaving my hometown in just five days, on a red-eye back to New York, where my life is now, but that doesn't mean that we can't enjoy the time we have left? Right?

Before I can process further, his body collides into mine, every ridge and cut muscle pressing firmly against me, taking me so completely off guard that my hands fist tightly into his shirt to hold on.

His lips move over mine with a sense of urgency, like if either of us were to blink, the moment would disappear.

I'm sure we both have the same reservations, only right now, with what we're feeling, neither of us cares.

My hands snake into his hair, grasping hold of the silky strands as he devours my mouth.

Claiming me.

The soft brush of his tongue against the seam of my lips has me whimpering against his touch, and he immediately pulls back, panting.

"Fuck, I'm sorry, Quinn…I don'-" he says quietly, taking a step back.

"Don't, don't apologize. I wanted you to," I say, cutting him off.

His gaze whips to mine. "You did?"

I don't give myself time to overthink, to convince myself that we shouldn't. Instead, I close the distance between us once more, sliding my arms around his neck. "I've wanted you to kiss me for a very long time, Dr. Grant, and I think we should worry less about what could happen and just focus on right now."

A beat passes, where his deep brown irises hold mine,

searching for any hesitation I know he won't find.

"Fuck it," he murmurs, bringing his hands to my jaw and cradling it before dipping down to brush his lips against mine. "I've wanted to do this for so goddamn long, Quinn Scott. You have no idea."

He kisses me until I'm a breathless, panting mess. Once our bodies become tangled, a mess of arms and legs, he hoists me up, his large hands palming my ass as my feet lock behind his back.

Only then, do I see a side of Parker that I've never known. A rough and dominating side of him.

My back hits the door in his hallway so hard, it rattles. Suddenly, Parker tears his mouth from mine, trailing kisses down my neck. Each one hotter than the last, burning a path that has me heating from the inside out.

My inner teenage self is currently having a field day with this. Parker Grant.

Dr. Parker Grant!

God, I basically had a shrine in my room dedicated to him. Okay, maybe not, but seriously, there was a time I couldn't imagine being with anyone besides him.

I tug at the unruly strands of his hair as he kisses and nibbles along my neck, gently grazing his teeth along my collarbone. The only exposed skin that he can, since I decided to wear this ridiculous sweater that currently has me sweating so badly, I may need an actual shower before any fun activities can truly happen.

"Fuckin' sweater." He groans, dropping his forehead against my chest. My giggle erupts before I can stop it.

"Well then, Dr. Grant…take it off." I wink.

When he lifts his head to stare into my eyes, I notice how his irises seem to blaze with what I can only assume is the same fire that he's lit inside me. Without words, I can feel the tension around us, the need. The desire.

I can feel how badly Parker wants me as he flexes his hips against me.

"Are you sure you want this, Quinn?"

I don't hesitate in my response, blurting it out before I lose the courage, "I'm *more* than sure. Fuck me, Parker. Please."

Never in my life have I been this brazen, but there's something about him that causes me not to care. I can't pinpoint it, but right now, it doesn't matter.

All that matters is feeling his lips on my skin, holding onto this feeling between us.

My words seemingly cause him to snap because he

grunts, hoisting me higher on his hips as he walks us toward the master suite, kicking the door open and then slamming it shut behind us. In two long strides, he tosses me down onto the bed, then climbs on top, his body hovering over mine.

Like this, I can feel every inch of his erection as it presses against me. Long and hard.

His lips find mine once more and he takes my mouth in a frenzy, my hands fisting in his shirt, his sliding underneath the thick hem of my sweater, along my stomach, and for a moment, I freeze.

What if he realizes that under this sweater is a girl who put on an additional twenty pounds once she moved to New York?

I've always been a curvier girl, and sure, Parker knows that but what if when he sees me naked, he changes his mind?

"What's wrong?" He pants, pulling back to look at me, taking his hand away as he does.

I sit up, pulling the sweater back down, and swallow thickly. I hate this conversation. The one where you have to warn someone about your body because they may not like it. The same conversation I have every time I date someone new, which is why I usually don't.

"I'm not skinny, Parker. I've seen the women you date. Well, at least the women you used to date, and I want to make it clear that under this sweater, there isn't a firm tummy or pointy hip bones."

He looks at me introspectively for a moment, saying absolutely nothing, and now I'm suddenly embarrassed.

"Come here," he commands, and my body willingly responds without question.

I scoot closer, but obviously not close enough, since he hauls me even closer and cradles my face tenderly in his hands. "You are fucking perfect, Quinn. You have always been perfect. I love every single goddamn inch of your curves. You hear me?"

His eyes hold mine, and I can see the promises in them. The sincerity.

My throat is suddenly tight. Emotion makes it hard to breathe, let alone form words.

"I hear you." My words are quiet, and when I avert my gaze, he uses his fingers to tip my chin up to look at him.

"If you only knew how many times I've fantasized about this. Fuck, every time I came as a teenager, it was your name on my lips. This is not new for me, love. I've wanted you since we were kids."

His words shock me speechless. What do I say to *that*?

"Let me show you, Quinn. I want to show you just how perfect you are…with my actions, not just my words."

With that, I nod and reach for him, my hands grasping the soft fabric of his Henley between my fingers as he kisses me. This time, slower and with intention. His hands slide from my jaw to the nape of my neck, where he gently holds me to him, sucking on my bottom lip, rolling it between his teeth, causing me to shiver.

Carefully, so tenderly that I feel like a precious object in his hands, he lays me back on his bed, dipping to where my sweater has risen, nuzzling the fabric up higher with his nose.

He pulls it up to my chest, exposing my breasts that are spilling from the cups of bright red lace. A pained groan leaves his lips, his eyes hungry on my pale skin. "Flawless."

Leaning forward, he kisses the soft skin of my breast, brushing the rough pad of his thumb over my lace-covered nipple, already a taut peak.

I'm wound so tightly that I feel like I'll combust at any given moment.

Seconds later, my sweater is pulled over my head and

discarded, leaving me bare from the waist up. Parker wastes no time, bringing his mouth back to my chest, as he reaches around and unhooks my bra, letting my breasts spill free.

"Fucking Christ, Quinn." He groans. His hands cup each one, squeezing gently, testing their heaviness as he leans forward and sucks a rosy pink peak into his mouth. Taking his time, he sucks, nips and lavishes each one with his tongue, peppering wet kisses along the swell then begins kissing a path downward.

Between my breasts, down to the valley of my stomach, and lower, until he's at the waistband of my jeggings.

Only then does he look up, and when I nod, another silent affirmation of permission, he hooks his fingers into the band and drags them down my legs.

Part of me still wants to cover myself, to hide from his gaze. Something that's been instilled in me for as long as I can remember, but I force myself to lie still as his eyes move down my body, unhurriedly.

When he pulls at the lace on my hips, tearing my underwear in one quick motion, I yelp in protest. "Parker!"

"Sorry, Quinny, I'll buy you another pair. A whole fucking drawer as long as you let me rip them off of you again." He grins, the tone of his voice betraying that he's not really sorry at all.

"I can tell how sorry you are. Now, it's your turn. I'm completely naked, and you're still fully dressed."

Parker pauses, sitting back slightly to gaze down at my naked body once more. "I want to worship you, Quinn Scott."

God, I'm melting like butter right now. He always seems to say just the right words to put me at ease.

My hands travel back to his face, where I cup his jaw, rubbing my thumb back and forth along the five o'clock shadow framing his face. I continue my path downward until I get to the top button of his Henley and pop it free.

The moment that my fingers brush along the hard muscles of his abdomen, he hisses, flexing forward against my already aching center. I drag my nails down, each muscle tightening with the movement, and then I push his shirt higher and higher, until he reaches behind his neck and pulls it off in one motion, tossing it to the side.

The light in the room consists only of pale moonlight, and it bathes us in its glow. Parker's body is a work of art. He must spend hours and hours at the gym to achieve this level of physique.

"I love seeing you look at me that way, love," he whispers hoarsely.

My eyes snap up to his, and I'm slightly embarrassed that I've just been caught checking him out so blatantly. But how could I not?

The man's body is nothing but sharp ridges and hardened planes, and I want to take my time acquainting myself with each one. I want to lose myself in his body, memorizing every inch of him.

Parker quickly ditches his jeans and boxers, then settles himself between my thighs. His big, hulking shoulders make me look almost small against him. Lowering my gaze, I see his cock bobbing against his stomach, hard and ready. To say that he's above average is putting it lightly.

No, Parker Grant's cock is *huge*.

There's no other way to say it, and for a second, I'm a little worried about whether or not it's going to fit. Long and veiny with a thick mushroom head.

My mouth literally waters at the sight of him. I want to taste him so badly.

In no hurry, he slides his hands up the outer parts of my thighs, and grips them in his hands. For once, I'm happy about my thick thighs.

Thank God I shaved my entire body before coming here today or this would've been embarrassing.

Parker dips his head between my thighs, rubbing the coarse hair of his stubble along the sensitive skin before dragging his nose along my folds and inhaling deeply.

"You smell so fucking good, Quinn." Using his fingers, he parts my lips, exposing my throbbing clit, and then flicks it with his tongue.

"Oh God," I cry.

In response, my back arches from the bed and my hands find his hair to pull him closer against me. Without warning, he spreads me wide open and begins devouring me like a starved man eating his last meal. Alternating between rough and fast strokes, he flicks my clit with his tongue, then takes it between his lips and sucks, flattening his tongue and licking me from ass to clit, over and over.

Nothing has ever felt so good. No one has ever brought me so close to orgasm so quickly, so effortlessly.

He circles his tongue around my entrance, spearing inside me, then replaces his tongue with his finger. While his tongue thrashes along my clit, he adds another finger, fucking me roughly. The sound is so erotic that goosebumps breakout along my arms, my nipples hardening as he tongue- fucks my drenched pussy.

"Fuck, you're so responsive, love. Come for me."

Just when I feel like I'm going to combust from the pressure of his fingers and the rhythm of his tongue, he rubs along my G-spot and my vision dances.

Black spots sparkle behind my eyes as my hands tug desperately at his hair. The pressure…it's too much.

I push back against the feeling, the sensation that I might pee, and let my orgasm take over. A sudden wet gush leaves my body as I tremble, my entire body quaking with the power of my orgasm, and through it all, he never stops his assault of my clit with his tongue. He brings it home, never letting up. Only when the tremors have subsided and I'm a panting, wet mess on the bed beneath him, does he pull back, leaving one last gentle kiss to my oversensitive clit.

"Holy fuck, that was incredible," he murmurs.

The reality of the situation sets in, and I sit upright, ready to scramble away.

Oh my god, did I just…squirt? On Parker? While his face was buried in my pussy? For the first time ever?

"Parker, I'm…" I trail off, unable to meet his eyes, "God, I'm so sorry."

"What do you have to be sorry for, Quinn? You just squirted all over my fucking face, and I've never seen anything sexier in my entire life. You have absolutely nothing to be sorry for. How about we do it again?" He smirks. My wetness is still glistening on his chin and lips, and everything about this moment has my body in overdrive.

It's so incredibly attractive that he's turned on by my body, by the taste of me. Picking up his discarded shirt, he wipes his mouth and pulls me to him for a kiss. I can still taste myself on his tongue, a musky sweetness that seems to linger in the kiss.

His kisses are languid and savory, as his tongue thrashes with mine. Somehow, we end up flat on his bed once more, this time his hips nestled between my parted thighs. The head of his cock nudges against my entrance, and a whimper escapes me.

Parker's lips are around my nipple, sucking and teasing the sensitive flesh, and it's enough to drive me wild.

"Need you, please," I beg.

He pulls back, letting go of my nipple with a pop, and his lust hazed eyes meet mine. This is happening. My head is clear, the haziness from the earlier eggnog gone, my thoughts laser-focused on him.

There's nothing I want more. I want him inside me. I want to be full of him.

Parker sees the look in my eyes, the expression on my face. He must see my need because he pulls back and reaches for a condom in the bedside table next to me, but my hand on his forearm stops him.

"I…I'm on birth control, and I'm one hundred percent clean. It's also been a while for me," I say, "if you want to… you know, go without one."

"Fuck, Quinn. There's nothing more in the world I want than to fuck you bare." He curses, lowering his head to take my mouth again. The kiss turns frantic, neither of us wanting any distance from the other. My hands rake down his arms as he tweaks my nipple between his fingers, rolling it roughly.

"Now, please."

Reaching between us, I fist his cock in my hand for the first time, my fingers barely closing around his length and pump gently, then harder when his hips rock into me. I guide him to my entrance and his hand covers mine. Together, we drag the blunt head of his cock through my wetness.

My clit throbs in sync with the pounding in my heart. Each time he circles my nub with his cock, I clench, desperate to have him inside me.

Parker lines his cock up with my entrance then thrusts inside me in one flex of his hips, driving himself to the hilt. I'm so full of his cock that I cry out, my chest arching against his waiting lips.

Slowly, torturously slow, he pulls out of me then thrusts back inside with a hard slap of his hips. He pulls my foot up to his broad muscled shoulder, so he can swivel his hips deeper, reaching a part of me that I never knew existed until this very moment.

Nothing and no one compares to him. There's only Parker.

With my foot on his shoulder, and my leg hoisted high in the air, he begins to fuck me furiously. His thrusts are punishing, and so deep that I can feel the head of him nudging against my cervix. So deep that it hurts just the smallest amount, but mixed with the pleasure, it sends me to euphoria. His strong, powerful body hovers over me as he fucks me enough to bring me to the brink of another mind-blowing orgasm, even without him touching my clit.

"I'm..." I can't even finish the sentence as he pounds

into me, harder and faster with each thrust.

"Come for me, Quinn. I want to feel you coming around my cock." He grunts, rutting into me, his intense eyes pouring into mine. Before he can even drop his thumb to my clit, I explode, fireworks detonating behind my vision for the second time tonight.

I come with him buried inside me, my body spasming and my back arching off the bed. Each drag of his cock in and out of me, sending me higher.

A different planet. An alternate universe.

It's indescribable. It's perfect.

"That's it, love, just like that." His brows are pinched in concentration, and I can tell by his expression, in the way that he plays my body that Parker isn't done.

Once the aftershocks of my orgasm have receded, he pulls out of my body, even as I protest, and lets out a hoarse laugh.

My eyes flit down to his cock, glistening with my juices, still harder than ever.

"You didn't come…" I pant.

"Because I'm just getting started, Quinn. Get on your stomach."

His hand lands against my ass cheek with a deafening

crack that echoes around the room and leaves my skin on fire. One turns into two, and before I know it, he's flipping me onto my stomach in one swift, effortless move.

I take back what I said about there not being a non-gentlemanly bone in his body, because that bone is definitely his cock. Who knew he would turn into this dirty…filthy talking man.

His fingers grip the soft skin at my hips, hauling my ass upward and back toward where he kneels behind me. Using his leg, he pushes my knees apart, and with his free hand, he wraps a fist around my now-wild hair. All of these things, combined with the feel of his cock teasing my entrance, has me feeling like I could explode. Like the barest brush of his fingers could send me tumbling back over the edge yet again.

My nipples, sensitive and raw from his mouth, brush along the bed, causing goosebumps to erupt along my skin.

"Parker," I moan, as he guides his cock through my drenched center, focusing on my throbbing clit, "Please."

"Fuck, I love to hear you beg."

With that, he slams back inside me so hard that it forces me up toward the headboard. My hands fist in the bedding as he fucks me, holding on for leverage, the soft fabric of his sheets muffling the cries that tumble from my lips as I press my face into the bed.

Just when I think I can't take another moment, another single ounce of pleasure, he lowers his hands between us and uses his thumb to massage my clit, and my orgasm hits me so suddenly and so unexpectedly hard that I collapse on the mattress with a strangled cry.

"Fuck, Fuck. Fuck," he grunts, slamming in deep, letting himself go. His big hands squeeze my ass cheeks, spreading them apart as he comes inside me. I can feel the warmth of his cum as it lashes inside.

His thrusts slow, and his fingers dance along my spine as he holds himself inside me until he begins to soften and then gently pulls out of me. He pads to the bathroom, only to return with a warm rag.

"Don't be sweet, Parker." I groan, turning over to lie on my back. But he ignores me and spreads my thighs, dragging the warm, damp cloth over my overly-sensitized pussy, cleaning the stickiness from between them.

Once he's done, he tosses the rag into the laundry bin and crawls back into bed, looping his arms around me and hauling me against his strong chest.

I don't bother saying anything else, because truthfully, I'm not even sure what to say.

We both just crossed into territory that we can't come

back from, and I'm not even sure if I want to.

Chapter Four
QUINN

"I'M ALL 'PEOPLE'D' OUT FOR THE NIGHT.
ACTUALLY, FOR THE REST OF THE YEAR. I'LL TRY AGAIN NEXT YEAR."
– QUINN SCOTT

MAREN MOORE

"I accidentally slept with Parker." I word-vomit the second my best friend Cassie answers my FaceTime call.

Her eyes widen, and her jaw drops. *"You did what?"*

Realizing she screeched so loud, the entire office probably heard her, she lowers her voice and looks around quickly. "As in…your brother's best friend, and the man you've been pining over since you were a teenager?"

"Yes, Cassie, the only Parker there is. That Parker. THE Parker. Dr. Parker Grant. The guy who fixes boo-boos for a living and helps old women cross the street."

I flop down onto my mom's couch, acutely aware that my entire body is sore in the most *delicious* way.

Thank God she's at the grocery store or this conversation would not be possible. Stacy's hearing is like a hawk, and the mention of a man would send her running.

"How did this accidentally happen? Obviously, you didn't just trip and fall onto his dick."

"Obviously. It was more of a slow descent." I grin when she rolls her eyes. It is sort of the truth, though. It's not as if we planned to have a mind-blowing one-night stand together. It just kind of happened, and I don't regret a single second of it.

Didn't mean he was going to win the bet though. I'm still staunchly anti-Christmas…but I'm all for sex.

"Well, it started with him dressing up like a sexy lumberjack. Okay, he wore an old henley and these worn jeans that hugged his butt, and I was trying my hardest to focus on the task at hand, which just so happened to be helping him decorate his Christmas tree, but then there was this moment…Ugh, I don't know, Cassie. He's so hot."

Cassie shakes her head, her long red hair falling around her in a curtain. "You're going to be back in New York in less than a week, Quinn. This is a horrible idea. What if you start to get deeper feelings for him?"

My brow furrows at her words. "Absolutely not. Never happening. First of all, I'm stronger than that. Second of all, it's just sex. Meaningless, albeit incredible sex. Nothing is stopping me from getting on that plane and coming home after the obligatory holiday activities, okay?"

She doesn't look convinced, but she nods anyway. "I've got to get back to work. Three more days till I'm out of here until the New Year. Keep me updated, okay? And please for the love of Father Christmas, think with your brain not your vag. 'Kay?"

"Got it." I give her a little salute and end the call, tossing my phone next to me on the couch cushion as I mull over her words.

Just because two adults have consensual, mind blowing sex does not mean feelings have to be involved.

A few minutes later, my phone buzzes. I glance down and see Parker Grant's name across the screen and sit up abruptly.

Can't stop thinking about you after last night. Pick you up at 8 for day two?

Day two?

I groan and drop back against the couch. Already another Christmas torture date?

I don't even begin to attempt to dissect that he's thinking about me. We need to have a clear conversation about what last night was, and wasn't, which leads to my short reply.

See you then.

I spend the rest of the day with Mom and Owen, putting up all of the outdoor decorations, including a ten-foot-tall inflatable Santa, complete with all eight reindeer and Rudolph leading the bunch. By the time we're done, I'm disgusting and covered in mud, and my boots are completely soaked through.

I rush upstairs and take a quick shower, making sure to exfoliate and shave every part of my body that I can reach, just in case I somehow accidentally end up having another night of mind-blowing sex with Parker, then take my time curling my hair and applying makeup.

Not that I have any intention of doing that again. I think.

I have no idea what Parker has in store for tonight, so I pick out a pair of jeans and a thick sweater paired with boots that hit my knees.

I throw on my coat and a scarf, then grab a beanie to shove in my bag. It's started to snow again, a thick white layer of fluff coating the ground, the temperature outside dropping.

When it's almost eight, I come downstairs and find Mom, Owen, and Cary at the dining room table, playing a game of Scrabble.

"Where are you off to this late?" Owen asks, a devious smirk on his face that reminds me of when we were teenagers.

"I'm meeting a friend for dinner."

"At eight o'clock?" he says skeptically.

Mom shushes him, shaking her head. "Owen Michael, leave your sister alone. I swear, you treat her like she's still a kid. She's all grown-up now."

I cross my arms over my chest. "Yes, at eight o'clock, if you must know. I'll be back later. Don't wait up."

Just as I'm about to slam the front door shut, I hear Mom call, "Your curfew is one o'clock, honey!"

As if she didn't just tell my brother to stop treating me like a child. Jesus Christ, I'm an *actual* adult.

I shouldn't be surprised, even if I am an adult. Owen's been my protector for my entire life, and obviously will not be stopping, even when I'm in my forties.

Thankfully, Parker's truck pulls up to the curb at exactly eight o'clock, saving me from freezing on the porch.

He comes around the truck, his hands shoved into his pockets, and looks up at me with a blinding smile that has my heart stuttering in my chest.

Leaning against the passenger side, he crosses his arms over his chest and waits for me to make it down the driveway to him.

"Hi," I say breathlessly from the pitter-pattering of my heart.

I shouldn't be this affected by his presence. Parker Grant makes me feel like a teenager again, stirring up old feelings and causing my heart to race in my chest.

"Hi," he replies, pulling me to him and planting a chaste kiss on my cheek before opening the passenger door for me to slide in. Once he's inside, he turns to look at me, pulling the gray beanie from his head.

"Loving Christmas yet, Quinny?"

"You wish."

Laughing, he turns the truck on, puts it in drive and pulls onto the street heading south. We ride in a comfortable silence, neither of us feeling the pressure to make conversation.

"Can we t-"

"So about last-"

We both start at the same time.

I laugh, turning to face him as he lets out a low, raspy chuckle that I feel in the pit of my stomach.

"Yes, I'd like to talk about it," he says finally. I want him to look at me, but I also like that I can observe his profile. The strong slope of his sharp jaw, the thick muscles in his neck. The dust of stubble along his jaw that runs down his neck.

I love it like this. It makes him look even more rugged, more like the lumberjack that I joked about with Cassie.

Truthfully, I like him casual like this, almost as much as I like him in a jacket and tie.

"Look, if you want to pretend it never happened, I'm fine with it and won't be hurt whatsoever. I don't want to make things weird or awkward between us, especially since you're Owen's best friend. People have one-night stands all the time, and we could be those people. Bang and never talk about it ever again," I say, simply.

What surprises me is that Parker looks almost… offended by what I've said. The crease between his brow deepens, and his jaw steels.

Suddenly, he pulls off to the side of the highway, parking the truck along the shoulder. He slams the gearshift in park, then turns to face me.

"That's not what I want, Quinn. And quite frankly, it pisses me off that you're so willing to brush last night off as if it's nothing." His jaw clenches and his throat bobs as he averts his gaze out to the darkness in front of us that's illuminated by the headlights.

Wait, what?

"I just…I figured…Okay, what are you saying, Parker?" I ask, trying to understand what is actually happening here.

I thought Parker and I sleeping together was a one-time thing, one that he would never want to even bring up again, and now I'm realizing that maybe we're on two completely different pages.

"Last night was not just a random hook-up for me, Quinn." He leans forward as he speaks, and I get a whiff of the musky cedar of his body wash, greedily inhaling his scent. I can't help it.

The man smells entirely too delicious for his own good. And he's making it hard to concentrate.

"There's no way that I can only have you once. Fuck no, Quinn. All I can think about is the way you taste." He leans closer, unbuckling the seat belt with a noisy clank as it hits the side of the truck. His hand grips my side, hauling me to the middle seat with no effort at all. "The way your tight, little body moved on top of mine while I was buried inside you."

When he leans forward, his lips just barely brushing against mine, all rational thought leaves my head.

Parker has a way of undoing me, unlike anyone else can.

"So maybe a repeat is necessary," I whisper, bringing my hands to the back of his neck and lightly tugging at the soft hair of his nape. "Maybe we shouldn't pretend it never happened."

"Hell no, we're not pretending, Little Scott." Parker lifts me off the seat and pulls me into his lap, settling me over his hardening length.

God, this…whatever this is…feels entirely too good to walk away from.

I slam my lips into his, drinking in the deep groan, and immediately tug at his hair to pull him closer. My hips rock against him, seemingly of their own accord, desperate for friction.

"Quinn, love, wait," Parker says as he pulls back, his chest heaving, much like my own. "As much as I want to strip you bare and take you right here, we're on the side of the road and it's snowing. Not safe. Plus, we're going to be late. Come back to my place with me tonight? We can talk about things there."

I sit back against the steering wheel and adjust my sweater that has risen up to my stomach, making me realize that we seriously just dry humped each other on the side of a major highway.

This is crazy.

And...I kind of love it.

"Sure. But I do think we need to have a conversation about this," I gesture from my chest to his, "and I think you may need to sit on the other side of the room while we do. I can't exactly think when you're this...distracting."

He flexes his hips at the word, and my brows rise, as if to say, see? Told you.

I somehow untangle myself from his lap and scramble back to my seat, a lot less put together and a whole lot hornier than I was before this happened.

Once I'm buckled back into the seat, Parker pulls the truck back on the highway, and this time, he keeps his hand on my knee for the remainder of the ride. The short stop seemingly washed away all the uneasiness between us.

Finally, he pulls the truck into a crowded parking lot that I would recognize anywhere.

"You're taking me ice skating at Moe's?" I squeal excitedly. "God, Parker, I haven't been here in so long. Since high school."

He grins, the corners of his lip tugging up slightly in a half grin. "I know. You used to love ice skating. Stacy would make us take you at least twice a month during the winter. We'd skate until we couldn't feel our faces then overdose on sugar from the hot cocoa. Figured you needed to be reminded of it."

Those are some of my favorite memories. When I was still learning to skate, Parker would stand in front of me and skate backwards while I held his hands. He always did his best to keep me upright, and without him, I would've had a lot more bumps and bruises.

"I'm *so* excited. I'll probably fall flat on my ass since I haven't skated in years and years, but oh well."

Parker gets out of the truck, then walks around to open my door. "I think it's a lot like riding a bike. You might not be as bad as you think. Maybe just a little rusty."

He takes my hand and tugs me toward the entrance, and in this exact moment, I realize just how different things are than what I expected my short trip home to be. The last thing I imagined was going on a date with Parker; yet, here we are, and it's not so bad.

We walk through the entrance, and I smile widely.

It hasn't changed a bit. It looks exactly like it did when we were teenagers, and my heart feels…fuzzy and warm.

Oh god, I'm turning into Parker. His cheerful Christmas crap is spreading, like a disease. Help.

"Let's get some skates," he says, guiding me toward the counter. As we walk over, I see the bench that I had my very first kiss on. Like I could ever forget that moment. Owen and Parker were there the second Adam Santino's lips touched mine. Apparently, Adam bet someone ten dollars that he could be the first to kiss me, and when they found out about it, they gave him a black eye and dared him to ever touch me again.

A memory I will not be forgetting in this lifetime or the next.

"What size?" Parker asks, jolting me from the memory. "Skate."

Shaking my head, I pull myself from the past. "Uh, a seven. I think. Thanks."

His brow furrows, and a curious expression ghosts

across his face. "What's that look for?"

"What look?"

"The one where you look like you just tasted spoiled milk." He extends the pair of worn and scuffed cream color ice skates out for me to take, then grabs his own pair from the clerk, and together, we begin walking over to the bench. I sit and take off my boots, then begin working on lacing the ice skates.

"I was just thinking about the day that you and Owen beat up Adam Santino because he bet everyone ten dollars he could kiss me."

Parker's expression hardens. "He was an asshole. The entire school knew it but you. I should've held him down and let *you* punch him."

My laugh echoes around us. "I'm pretty sure there was no way that Owen was letting him walk away that day without two black eyes and a busted nose."

"Yeah, you're probably right."

It takes me longer than it normally would to get my feet in the skates and get them laced up correctly, so Parker kneels down in front of me and makes quick work of them. He fastens them tightly, then stands and holds out his hand for me. "Ready to do this, Quinny?"

"Ready as I'll ever be."

We head straight for the rink, and the moment that I step foot on the ice, it's like all of the muscle memories from the time we spent at the rink come flooding back. Parker was right. It is a lot like riding a bike, except ice skating is even easier for me than riding a bike.

The smooth ice glides beneath my skates, and I'm lost in the nostalgia of it all. I do a quick spin that almost has me falling on my face, and then turn to face Parker.

He's grinning, and the slow clap that follows is as embarrassing as it is flattering.

"Told you that you'd be great. I can't imagine anything that you wouldn't be great at, Quinn."

His words hit me directly in the pit of my stomach, and I melt, skating back in front of him and placing my hands on the thick material of his jacket.

"Thank you for taking me back here, Parker. It's the little things like this that I miss about home, and I guess I just didn't realize how much until I came back. I mean…I could skate back home in New York, but it wouldn't really be the same. Not that I have time to do anything but work. My boss thinks it's a sport to work me until I'm falling asleep at my desk."

My feet glide forward, taking me a few feet away from Parker, who's watching me with a stormy look in his bright eyes.

"And you like that? Your job?" He skates up and takes a spot next to me with ease as we begin to skate in circles around the rink, side by side.

His question makes me pause. Do I *actually* like my job?

I guess, I like what I do, and I've busted my tail to achieve a lot professionally. But the job itself? No. It's terrible. My boss, my work environment, the grind… everything about it is terrible. But I earned the promotions I have by working hard and putting my career first, sacrificing what I had to in order to get where I am.

Even if I hated it, I earned it.

"I like what I do. I love marketing. It's something that I've always been passionate about, and it made sense to finish my degree in it and find a job in the field. I just…I don't know if the firm that I'm at right now is going to work out long-term." That was something I'd not even admitted to myself until this moment.

Parker reaches out and takes my palm in his, lightly rubbing his thumb along the back of my hand as we find a steady rhythm skating together. It should feel weird holding his hand, but it doesn't. It feels right, and I try not to think about that for too long.

"Why not?"

"Because my boss is an asshole. God, I remember when I got the offer to work there, Parker. I was over the moon. I was in a new city, freshly graduated from college, and I felt like I had the entire world at my fingertips. They offered me competitive benefits and a salary the size I'd never expected. I couldn't wait to work there. Then I started and quickly realized that the only way I was going to be taken seriously at this firm was if I worked ten times harder than everyone else. Particularly, all the men."

Parker scoffs. "Quinn, you've always been the toughest girl I've ever known. Hell, you used to give guys twice your size so much shit, they never messed with you again. I can imagine you handled all those fuckers quick."

If he only knew the things I had to do to be taken seriously, to prove that women are just as capable as men. In this century, it's hard to believe that we're still living in olden times and women don't have the same rights as men.

"It's been interesting. I can say, without a doubt, that I've earned my spot at this firm. I just don't think that it's where I'm meant to be long-term. More of a stepping stone in the path of my career. I'd love to open my own firm one day. Be my own boss and build my own team. Work with the clients that I choose."

"You could do that, you know? Why wait? I think that you could do anything that you put your mind to. I've seen you do it before, and no one is in charge of your future but you."

I laugh and shake my head, gently bumping my shoulder into his as we come around the large curve of the ice rink. "I'm thinking you've become a master at motivational speeches since I left."

A hoard of kids fly by us, and one of the kids brushes against me by accident, causing my feet to fly out directly from underneath me. Flailing, I reach out and grab hold of Parker, who somehow manages to keep us both upright, while I try to catch my balance.

"Woah," he says, steadying me in his strong arms. They wrap around me, holding me to his chest.

I could blame the thundering of my heart on the fact that I almost fell face first on the ice, but I know that it isn't that at all. It's Parker's hands on me, causing me to come alive beneath him.

"S-sorry, that kid…" I trail off, my train of thought

completely lost as Parker's breath hitches, and he moves in closer.

I can feel the warmth of his breath as it dances along my lips. A centimeter more and they'll brush mine. My eyes flutter closed, and I wait, my fists clutched in his jacket while he still holds me.

Then, another kid zooms past, sending us both falling into the sideboards.

"Shit, are you okay?" he says quietly, checking me all over.

"I'm okay. Just a bump. I won't break, Parker." I laugh. "Although, I'm pretty sure the day I broke my arm here in third grade, you cried more than I did."

Parker blanches, pulling back with wide eyes. "You said you would never bring that up ever again, Quinn Scott. You fucking swore it."

I shrug. "It was a Christmas I will never forget. I'm pretty sure you felt so bad the entire time I had a cast on that you would bring me endless hot cocoas with whipped cream and sprinkles."

"You were hurt, and I was worried about you. I would've done anything you asked that month. Remember what I got you for Christmas?" he asks.

Like I could ever forget.

I wasn't exaggerating when I said that so many of my childhood memories include him, at least the ones that stand out.

Taking my hand, he holds it protectively in his as we circle the rink again, our skates gliding on the smooth ice.

"You bought me a bell. It was so loud, my mom said if I rang it one more time, she was tossing it right into the trash. But every time I rang it, you came running." I laugh, tossing my head back as I think about how quickly he would round the corner into our kitchen, if I so much as touched that bell. I guess I never truly noticed how attentive and caring Parker was when it came to me back then. I was always the kid sister, or at least I thought.

"Eh, I was a softy. I've hardened in my old age."

He shoots me a wink, then drops my hand and skates ahead, making zigzags in the ice with his skates.

I'm pretty sure if I attempted that, I would definitely end up face down on the ice.

Good thing I've got a hot doc to nurse me back to health.

"Come on, see if you can spin like you used to?"

Even though I worry I might end up on my ass, I

attempt the move that once came so easy to me. We spend the next hour chasing each other on the ice and touching each other every chance we get, until both of our noses are red and frozen.

"Ready for some hot chocolate? Pretty sure my fucking toes are going to freeze off." He laughs, offering me his hand.

"Yes, please."

Hand in hand, we exit the ice and find a small table tucked away from the noise. I sit and wait for Parker to come back with the hot chocolate, and when he does, I could almost cry. All my fingers and toes are practically frozen, and I can't wait to drink the sugary goodness that he's carrying over.

"Thank you," I say, as he sets the cup down in front of me then takes the seat beside me, draping his arm across the back of my chair. "You know, I think that this hot chocolate may even be better than Grandma Scott's eggnog. It's a tough call, but seriously, I don't know how they make it this damn good."

I take a long sip of the hot drink, swirling it around in my mouth as I savor the chocolatey flavor. So milky, so sweet, so good. I look around, warming from the hot chocolate and all the action around me, then I suddenly see something out of the corner of my eye that grabs my attention.

"Is that...*Santa Claus?*"

Parker glances back to where I'm now staring and sees that it is, indeed, the jolly, fat man dressed in a full suit with a large velvet sack thrown over his shoulder. It seems like no one else has realized he's here yet because he's alone.

"Looks like it. C'mon, gotta tell him what you want for Christmas." Parker grins, tugging me up from the chair before I can protest.

When was the last time I saw someone actually dressed as Santa? I mean, besides the people who ring bells on the sidewalk to raise money for charities, but usually that's just a guy in a way too big costume, who doesn't nearly look the part.

But this guy?

He could actually pass for the real Old Saint Nick. His midsection is full and robust, the black belt around his waist is on the last loop and he fills out the suit perfectly. The red in his cheeks is authentic, not painted on, but what really sells it? The thick, fluffy white beard and hair that frame his chubby cheeks. The red and white velvet Santa hat falls to the side, and the poofy white ball at the end bounces with each step he takes.

"Did you set this up?" I ask Parker, as I breathlessly try and keep up with him. "As a part of our bet? Playing dirty Santa on me, Dr. Grant."

"Nope, I swear. This was complete serendipity, but we're going to take advantage of it."

With Parker's fingers tightly entwined with mine, he leads the way to Mr. Claus.

By the time we cross to the other side of the rink, Santa's set his bag down. The thick gold rope still secure, keeping it tightly closed, and he's taken a seat at an empty table.

"Hi," Parker says to him, extending his free hand for Santa to shake.

When he looks up, his entire face seems to light up, a warm smile spreading on his lips.

Something warm and fuzzy inside me seems to be happening again, only stronger this time, and I'm not prepared for it. But what kind of person would I be if I was unhappy to see Santa Claus?

I'm not that much of a grump.

Am I?

I don't even have time to think about the question I've posed for myself because Santa stands and pulls me into his arms in a warm, inviting hug then he chuckles.

"Well, Merry Christmas!" Pulling back to look at me, he says, "Would you like a photo?"

My eyes dart to Parker, who's looking entirely too smug standing to the side, his arms crossed over his chest, wearing a satisfied grin. He's enjoying this way too much.

"Uh, I…" I stammer.

"She would love a photo. And she'd *love* to tell you what she wants for Christmas."

I'm going to kill him.

"*We'd* like a picture together," I say, narrowing my eyes. Parker only laughs and waltzes over with an annoying amount of pep in his step. "And I think I'm a *bit* too old for that."

Santa scoffs, like me saying that I'm too old to sit on his lap and tell him what's on my Christmas list is just too absurd. "Nonsense. No one is ever too old to sit with Santa. Right, young man?"

His question is directed at Parker, and, of course, he agrees with a non-committal shrug. "What could it hurt?

This one is in desperate need of some Christmas cheer, Santa. Go on, Quinn, tell him what it is that you want for Christmas this year."

I can tell that neither of them is going to let this go, so I sigh and suck it up, making my way to sit *next* to 'Santa' because something tells me that Parker is obviously set on this.

He keeps his phone out, aimed toward the two of us, and if the daggers I'm currently shooting him were real, he'd be ten feet in the grave by now.

"What is it you'd like for Christmas?" Santa asks, a hearty chuckle leaving his lips, "Anything is possible…if you believe."

Jesus, give me a break. Please, if there ever was a time. Let this be my own Christmas miracle and put me out of my misery.

"All I want for Christmas is for my family to be happy."

"That's it?" he says, the crease between his brow wrinkling with the question.

"That's it."

Santa smiles. "You're a good girl, Quinn Scott, and you have a good heart. Remember sometimes it's okay to want things for yourself too."

"Thank you. This was...it was great. Merry Christmas," I say, rising from the seat next to him. Before Parker can subject me to anymore torture, I grab his hand and pull him toward the rink's exit.

Once we're outside of the double doors, the freezing night air upon us, only then do I realize...I never told Santa my last name.

Chapter Five
QUINN

"I'M JUST OVERLY EXCITED FOR THE FAT MAN TO VISIT."
- QUINN SCOTT

How many orgasms can a girl have before she dies? This is a legitimate question that I'm in dire need of an answer to. Parker's given me more orgasms in a single night than I've had with another man in...*years*. I'm so sore that I can hardly move, but at least we had time to recover when he brought pie to bed and forced me to watch *The Grinch* until I fell asleep halfway through on his chest.

Now, the last thing I want to do is leave our little bubble of mind-blowing sex to go to dinner with my family. I've been dreading this since the moment my mother brought it up. Although, I'm sure it's going to be quite entertaining having all of us in one place, sharing a meal. I can't remember the last time that happened. But this year, Mom is hellbent on bringing us all together to spend the holidays, and that includs my father and his new wife.

"Ready for this?" Owen asks, taking a seat across from me, straightening the tie around his neck as he does.

Not only are we going to have to suffer through the stuffiest Christmas dinner of all time, we have to do so all dressed up.

Which means that I had another opportunity to break out the new Louboutins, so I guess it isn't ALL bad after all.

"I guess. Hopefully he leaves early." I pick up the glass of wine in front of me and swirl it around absentmindedly before taking a hefty sip. I can't help but notice that Parker hasn't touched his.

The one good thing about tonight?

We're sitting next to each other.

"Be nice, Quinn. Can't we all have a nice, calm dinner together? Your father and I have been working really hard to leave things in the past in order to come together for the holidays. We all need to try," Mom chides.

It takes everything I have not to roll my eyes. Instead, I take another sip of my wine and sag back against the chair.

She's right.

Wooosah, Quinn.

Under the table, I can feel the heat of Parker's hand as

he slides it along my knee, causing me to jump in surprise. His fingers squeeze gently, offering me reassurance, and somehow, I relax. I can actually feel the tension leave my body.

I glance over at him and his face is a mask of attentiveness as he listens intently to the story Owen is telling about his job. His gaze never leaves Owen's, nodding along, all while sliding his hand up my thigh a centimeter at a time.

His handsome profile is unwavering, but me? Well, my entire body is reacting to his touch.

Which is both terrifying and thrilling at the same time.

"Quinn?" my mother calls, jolting me from the feel of Parker's hand.

I clear my throat, flustered. "Yeah? Sorry."

"I swear I called your name three times. I said your father's here."

I nod and set my wine glass down on the table, sucking in a deep, calming breath. Owen and Cary stand and walk out of the room to greet him, leaving Parker and me alone.

The moment that they're gone and I stand from the chair, his hand meets the small of my back as he speaks, "Are you okay?"

"Yes. I'm fine. Just…nervous. About seeing my dad. It's been a while, and things are kind of strained."

"I understand. But I'm here if you need me, okay?"

I give him a small smile as I nod. "Thank you."

Together, we walk into the foyer, and I see my dad standing with his new wife, Maria.

He looks older since the last time I saw him. There are deep set lines at the corners of his eyes, and his crow's feet are more pronounced.

A spot in my heart aches at the sight of him. A part of me, the little girl who needed her dad, she yearns to reach out and bridge the gap between us.

If only it were that easy. If it were, years wouldn't have gone by so quickly.

He's wearing a dark gray sports jacket, with a pressed white-button down and slacks. His wife is in a dark navy dress, her long blonde hair gathered to the side with a ruby diamond clip.

She's beautiful, even if I hate to admit it.

"Quinn," My dad says softly, stepping hesitantly toward me. I can see the longing and adoration on his face as he looks at me, and guilt suddenly claws at my throat.

"Hi," I whisper, unsure of what to even do or say right

now.

He steps forward and pulls me in for a hug, lingering for a moment before stepping back next to Maria.

I hold out my hand for her to shake, and she bypasses it altogether, gathering me in a tight, quick hug, like we've known each other for years without an ounce of awkwardness.

It's completely unexpected, and for some reason, it causes me to tear up.

"Hi, Quinn. I've heard so much about you. It's so nice to finally be able to spend time together," she whispers in my ear before pulling away.

"Uh, yes, me too."

She smiles warmly and rejoins my father by his side. My mother then sweeps back into the room and starts giving instructions. I notice that her interaction with my father isn't anything like I remember it being. They both seem to have shelved their issues, and it makes it easier to sit down together without fear of a war happening.

Mom sits at one end, and Dad at the other. Maria is seated next to me, and Owen next to Dad. Parker next to Mom. I expected there to be an argument over appetizers, but it's quite the opposite.

Everyone is in a great mood, laughing and sharing old stories. Nothing like I expected it to be. Even Owen seems relaxed as he shoves mashed potatoes in his mouth with the main course.

"So, uh," my mother clears her throat quietly and sets her linen napkin down onto her plate once we've finished eating, "there is a reason your father and I wanted to have dinner together this Christmas."

She glances over at him with a small smile and nods slightly, signaling him to speak.

"We've been seeing a counselor, together, and with Maria, for the past few months. There were things that we needed to repair, both individually and together, for the sake of you two and for my marriage."

To say I'm shocked is an understatement. Of all the things I expected them to say...this is not it. Not even close.

Once more, I feel Parker's hand on my knee, squeezing reassuringly, as if he can read my mind. I need the physical touch more right now than I even realized. Reaching under the table, I grab his hand and lace it in mine, resting them on my lap.

"I think it's safe to say that we've let go of a lot of the

things that have been weighing both of us down for a long time. Right, Stacy?"

My mother nods, catching my gaze, then Owen's. "It was something that we had to do together, in order to move forward. We also wanted to apologize to you both. We know that things were hard...Back when we decided to divorce. You kids heard things that you shouldn't have, and that's something that both of us will have to live with. We just hope that we're able to move forward as a family, all in love and light."

After she finishes speaking, I look at Owen, who seems to be as shocked as I am. I truly don't even know how to process what she's just said.

My heart is thrumming inside my chest. *Is* that what I want? To move on?

To be a family again?

"I think I'd like to try," I whisper, my voice so full of emotion that it hardly even sounds like my own.

"Me too," Owen adds.

Both of our parents look happier than I've seen them in years, and I feel something inside me crack. Something broken and cold that I'd tucked away a long time ago.

I needed this. More than I could have ever known.

"We're going to start by making this a yearly thing," Mom says, "Getting together for the holidays, spending Christmas and Thanksgiving together. We're lucky to have each other and to have the ability to all be together for the holidays."

"I've missed you both, and I hope that we can work on our relationship to get it in a better place. I'm sorry for missing as much as I have. I'm sorry for allowing our relationship to be strained in the first place. After your mother and I divorced, I wasn't in a good place, and I have no one but myself to blame for my actions." My father looks at me, regret flashing in his eyes. The same regret that I feel deep in my bones for letting things get as badly as they have between us. We hardly even spoke anymore. The wedge between us only getting larger and larger as the time passed.

This is our chance to repair what's broken. I didn't realize that, deep down, I wanted this, and I pushed it aside because I was hurt.

"That means you have to come home more than once in four years, Quinn. No more of this, 'I'm too busy with work' excuse," Mom says, her eyes narrowing.

"I promise to try," I say, crossing my heart. "I'll make

an effort to come home more often, and in the event that I can't, I'll FaceTime."

Parker's fingers tighten around my knee ever so slightly, and I relax into the touch. It's his way of letting me know that he's here, and even though he can't say it out loud, he's supporting me.

This is the craziest week of my life, and it isn't even over yet. Who would've thought that I would be in bed with my brother's best friend, and that my parents would put aside their differences, so we could spend the holidays together?

It seems like an actual Christmas miracle. One that I didn't ask for, but gladly take regardless.

Chapter Six
QUINN

"CALL ME A SCROOGE. THE GRINCH.
THE GIRL WHO HATES CHRISTMAS."
        - QUINN SCOTT

❝Any reason you're walking around with an actual pep in your step, Quinn Scott?" Mom asks when I round the corner into the kitchen and steal the piece of peppermint bark out of her hand. My bag is hoisted high on my shoulder as I prepare for yet another night at Parker's.

With only a few days left before I'm headed back to New York, we agreed that we'd make the most of it, and Parker is not giving up on his crusade to defrost my cold Christmas hating heart.

I feign innocence and shrug. "No reason. You know, just overly excited for the fat man to visit."

She scoffs. "If only I didn't know better."

Her disbelief makes me smirk, and I just skate around the topic, steering it back to her event planning as Tony Bennett croons in the background.

"How's things down at the theater?"

"We're shaping up nicely, but don't worry, all you'll have to do is show up on opening night in your little elf costume and look pretty as you hold Santa's presents."

"Mkay. I've gotta run, but I'll see you...later?"

Stacy Scott is a lot of things, but a fool is not one of them. She looks at me skeptically, rolling her lips together. "You do know that I know exactly where you've been lately? Sneaking home in the middle of the night like your sixteen again."

"What do you mean?" Picking up her egg nog, I take a sip to wash down the peppermint bark.

"I'm your mother, Quinn Scott. I know everything, and I know that you and a certain doctor have been getting very cozy."

Mid drink, I spray the smallest amount of egg nog out at her mention of Parker, but somehow manage to swallow down the rest.

"Uh, not sure what you mean."

She sets down the peppermints she was crushing with the rolling pin and crosses her arms over her chest. "I told you, a mother knows everything, and it's not exactly like the two of you are very inconspicuous. You know that I love Parker, and he's like my own son. Just...be careful, Quinn. You have a life back in New York that doesn't include him, and I just don't want to see either of you hurt."

Her words sink in slowly, and I swallow down the emotion that is rising in my throat. She's not wrong...but part of me isn't really ready to think about walking away from Parker. I just want to enjoy the time we have left together, and then we can face reality.

"We're just friends, Mom. You know...Parker and me. We've always been friends. It's okay, kay?"

She doesn't look convinced at all, but she nods and holds out her arms for me to walk into them. When they slide around me, holding me against her small body, I sigh.

"Love you, Mom."

"Love you too, sweetheart. Always."

For a moment, we just stay like that, neither of us moving, neither ready to let go. No matter how old I get, or how far I move, I will always be a girl that needs her mom, and like now, sometimes a girl just needs a hug from her mom.

There's a honk outside, signaling Parker's arrival, so I pull back and smile. "I'll see you later, okay? Tomorrow,

we'll have a wrapping party and watch *A Christmas Story.*
Sound good?"

"Sounds good. Be careful."

Nodding, I swipe another piece of peppermint bark
and walk out the front door. Like yesterday, Parker's
leaning against his old truck with his arms crossed over
his chest, looking deliciously edible.

He's got on a pair of charcoal-colored slacks that hug
his muscular thighs and make my mouth water. They're
paired with a black button-down and a pair of black
loafers.

"You didn't tell me to dress up," I say to him, once I've
made it down the slick driveaway.

He reaches out and takes my bag off my
shoulder, slinging it over his, and then pulls me in for a
long, deep kiss. When he pulls back, I realize that my toes
have curled in the Uggs I'm wearing.

He has that effect on me.

"Not necessary. I just have to stop back at the office
real quick and look at some paperwork that needs a
signature. Figured now is as good of a time as any to show
you around. If you're up for it."

"Of course. I wish I could see you in action one day, Dr.

Grant."

The innuendo is not missed because his large hand slides to the small of my back and he yanks me to him, sealing his lips over mine before using his other hand to swat me on the ass. Hard.

"In the truck, Scott, before I change my mind and fuck you right here," he says, opening the passenger door for me to slide in.

"Really?" I say, once he walks around and joins me. "Are you ever *not* listening to Christmas music? I don't even know what kind of music you like anymore, since all I've heard is Mariah Carey blaring out of the speakers since I've been home."

Parker throws his head back and laughs. "What's better than Christmas music, Quinn?"

"I dunno…anything? Literally, anything."

"Stop being a scrooge. It's non-negotiable, love. Buckle up."

I cross my arms over my chest and pretend to pout before reaching up and quickly buckling. "Fine."

Parker pulls out onto the highway in the direction of his office, and as we drive, he cranks the music up, singing his own rendition of "Jingle Bells." Only this time, it's

Jingle Balls, and now I can't stop thinking about his balls.

I mean honestly, the guy has amazing balls. Not too small, not too large, and I particularly like them when they're in my mou-

"Quinn?"

My head whips to the side to look at Parker, and I realize that we've stopped. The headlights of his truck illuminate his practice, snowflakes falling sideways with the wind.

Hell, I was fantasizing about his balls, and I didn't even realize we had stopped.

"Yes. You were saying?"

"I was saying, we're here." He laughs lightly, shaking his head.

"Right, okay."

While Parker gets out and walks around to open my door, I unbuckle the seat belt, enjoying the last second of warmth before cold air hits me. I should be used to the cold by now, but it still takes me by surprise and chills me to the bone whenever I step outside.

"Come on, let's get inside. It's freezing." Parker guides me to the front door, then unlocks it with his key, ushering me inside. It's not much warmer inside the office, but at least we're out of the wind and snow.

He walks over to the light switches and flicks them on, illuminating the space. It's warm, and inviting and it honestly doesn't feel much like a doctor's office, which I know was the goal. The walls are painted a warm taupe color, with bright murals hanging on most of the walls, along with framed awards and certificates for Parker.

"Wow," I breathe, walking around the waiting room as I take everything in, "Parker, this is incredible. You should be so proud."

"Thank you. I'll give you the behind-the-scenes tour, come on." He holds out his hand, and without pause, I slide my palm in his and let him guide me around the office, showing me the patient rooms, the reception area, and then lastly, his office.

Painted a deep red, it feels like I'm stepping back in time. There's all wood and bronze finishings, and a dim lamp in the corner, casting a warm glow around the room. There are built-in book cases lining the walls, full of books. Medical journals. Files. A few awards scattered along them as well.

In the middle of the room sits a large oak desk, and a matching shelf behind it. The desk itself is clean, only a few files sit in the middle. When I walk around to look, I drag my fingers along the polished wood and smile when I see a framed photo of Owen and Parker on a fishing trip with Parker's dad, and then a photo of the three of us after our high school football team won the state championship.

"I can't believe you kept this picture after all this time," I say, my eyes lifting to his. He's starting intently, his hands shoved into the pockets of his slacks, as he leans against one of the bookcases.

"Of course I kept it, Quinn. Just because you left, doesn't mean that I was going to forget you," he says quietly, and my heart hammers inside my chest.

There are so many things that I left behind when I took off to New York, so many people. Parker included.

He strides over, takes the frame from my hand, and sets it back down, then pulls me against his chest with his arms wrapped tightly around my body. I can feel his lips press against the top of my hair. "I've got to work on this paperwork for a bit, then we'll head out, okay?"

I nod. "Of course. I'll catch up on the emails I've been neglecting."

Truth be told, I haven't even glanced at my email since landing in Strawberry Hollow. I told myself I was taking this week off completely, but the workaholic inside of me has been struggling not to check it.

I needed to unplug and untangle myself from my job, even if it was only temporarily.

It's been nice, not having to spend every waking moment with my eyes glued to my phone or my computer screen. And it's made me realize how much time I've spent working and not living. I've lived in New York for four years, and I hardly even know the city.

For the next hour, I scroll through social media, or at least pretend to. My eyes can't seem to stay off Parker as he works. Who knew that writing could be so sexy? He scans over each file, scribbling deftly onto each one, his brow furrowed in concentration.

Completely lost in his work.

Parker Grant is sexy on his own, but Dr. Grant? Well, that's a whole new ballgame. The energy he exudes…it commands the room.

After watching him work for ten more minutes and getting more turned on with each second that passes, I can't take it anymore. I toss my phone down on the leather couch I'm sitting on and quietly make my way over to his desk. I hoist myself up onto the side and let my feet dangle, toeing off my boots until they're both on the office's floor.

"Are you trying to distract me, Quinn?" he rasps as I snake my foot into his lap and over his cock, brushing against the fabric of his slacks.

Feigning innocence, I ask, "I dunno, is it working?"

Parker sets down the pen and leans back in his office chair, lacing his hands behind his head. "Maybe."

Maybe, huh?

Leaning forward, I drag my hand down the front of his dress shirt and over his rock-hard abdomen, until I reach the buckle of his pants. I hop off his desk to stand between his wide spread thighs and gently use my foot to push his chair back, so I can drop to my knees between them.

I reach for his buckle once more, quickly opening the belt then get to work on the button of his slacks. Once it pops free, I drag the zipper down, looking up at him through my mascaraed lashes, drinking in the lust-filled expression on his face.

He's so handsome, it sets my body on fire.

With the zipper lowered, I reach into his boxer briefs and wrap my fist around his cock. The moment my hand connects with his velvet hardness, he sucks in a sharp hiss.

"Quinn." He groans as I pump him slowly, using the

pad of my thumb to spread the precum beading around the head of his cock, paying special attention to the sensitive spot under it. Unable to waste another second, I lean forward and take him into my mouth, sucking gently, as my hands circle his cock, twisting along with the rhythm of my mouth.

I want to bring Parker Grant to his knees. I want him to remember this week, however short it may be. I want him to never be able to sit in this chair again without thinking about me on my knees, sucking his cock.

When his hands slide into my hair, fisting tightly, I take him deeper until he hits the back of my throat. With how deep he is, and his size, I can't help but gag slightly, only to be rewarded with a deep groan that erupts from his chest.

"Goddamnit, love. You look so good taking my cock."

The words tumble from his lips so breathlessly, so unbelievably hot, that it only makes me want to please him more.

The look of pure reverence on his face has me tumbling further into a pool of lust at his feet.

He looks like a god.

That's the only way to describe Parker in this moment.

I bob up and down on his cock, taking him as deep

as I can, letting the head of his cock bump the back of my throat, until he tugs at my hair, pulling my mouth off of him with a pop.

"I'm about to come, Quinn, and the only place I'm going to be coming is inside you," he says, standing abruptly from the chair and helping me off my knees. He reaches out and grabs my hand, tugging me to him.

"I told you once that your mouth was going to get you in trouble, but really, it seems like it's going to be what keeps you out of it," he whispers, leaning down to brush his lips along mine. "I can't wait another fucking second to be inside you."

Before I can even respond, he pulls me with him, out of his office, and into the room that neighbors his. It's a patient exam room, complete with an exam table.

Immediately, my mind turns all naughty and not nice, and I think of all the things I would like Dr. Grant to do to me on that table. Hmm.

I let go of Parker's hand and turn toward him, bringing the back of my hand to my forehead like a true actress. "Oh, Dr. Grant, I'm so sick." I cough dramatically through my words. "I think I need you to make me feel better."

Parker's eyebrows rise, and a grin tugs at his lips

before he clears his throat, and he quickly snaps into character.

"Well, Ms. Scott, I'd be glad to get you taken care of. But you have to understand that I have to do a very thorough exam in order to correctly diagnose the problem. You see, lots of sicknesses can present themselves as different things based on the symptoms."

Oh God. Who knew doctor talk could be this hot?

I'm ready to fling myself at him like a sex-crazed idiot, but instead, I bite my lip and nod. "Of course. Whatever it takes to get rid of this terrible...ache."

This is why I work in marketing and not Hollywood. I'm a terrible actress.

"Very well. Please have a seat on the exam table and start by removing your clothing," he says, walking over to the counter and grabbing a pair of gloves from the box. "For the exam."

While I'm removing my clothes, his eyes slowly skim my body, taking his time drinking in every inch. In all my life, I've never felt so exposed...so vulnerable. Yet the way that his eyes seem to burn with each piece that I remove gives me the confidence to continue.

Parker slides his large hands into the latex gloves and

is in front of me within two strides, peering down at me. Oh, so he's really playing the part.

"All of it, Ms. Scott."

Gulping, I quickly unhook my bra and let it fall free, then drag the boy shorts down my hips, leaving me completely bare for his gaze to feast upon.

"Thank you. Please have a seat on the exam table."

His tone is professional and curt, but underneath I can hear the restraint that he's scarcely holding onto.

I do as I'm told and lift myself onto the exam table, scooting backwards slightly. My nipples are hard and standing at attention from the cool draft in the room, or maybe because of Parker's gaze on me.

"If you'll lie back, I'll begin my exam."

His fingers trail seductively along the arch of my foot, up over my calves to the juncture of my thighs, where he barely brushes my center before continuing upward. It's impossible to remain still under his touch.

The best and worst type of teasing is feeling his fingers exploring my body.

"Tell me where it hurts, Ms. Scott," he says as he leans down, his hot breath fanning along the shell of my ear, causing goosebumps to erupt on my already chilled flesh.

Everywhere he touches seems to burn. A fiery path that only he's able to extinguish. A douse that only he carries.

"E-Everywhere." My voice comes out faint. I'm completely caught up in the moment, and I can hardly form any words.

Every part of me feels singed by his touch.

"Here?" he asks, trailing his fingers along the underside of my breast, brushing the pad of his gloved thumb over the sensitive peak of my nipple, causing me to arch into his touch.

"Yes."

Using both of his hands, he cups my breasts, rolling my nipples between his fingers and massaging them until my legs are pressed so tightly together that they begin to ache. Although, it's nothing compared to the ache inside me.

My eyes stay trained on him as he "examines" me, and I almost laugh at the serious expression on his face. He's concentrating so intently on my body.

"What about here?"

His fingers travel down my stomach to my thighs, where he opens them gently, his pupils dilating when he sees how wet I am from our game of pretend.

There's absolutely nothing fake about the way that I

want him.

"*Definitely* there."

The air surrounding us is so thick that it feels like it's hard to breathe. All I can concentrate on is the feel of his hands on me, the way that he murmurs appreciatively when he spreads my thighs wider.

"I'll see what I can do to make it feel better." He husks, grazing his thumb along my throbbing clit before circling it. My nails dig into the table as he rubs and my entire body goes into overdrive with each stroke of his finger. "I need to see what the problem is."

I find myself nodding, over and over, until I feel the cool air hit my clit, and his fingers are gone. He situates himself on the stool at the end of the exam table and spreads me open, eyeing my most sensitive parts with intent.

"You have the prettiest pussy I've ever seen, love," Parker mutters low and hoarse. "I could stare at it all day."

The rubber exam gloves on his hands disappear in the blink of an eye, and he seals his mouth over my clit, sucking hard, sliding his fingers inside me and roughly fucking me with them.

"Oh God, Parker." I pant, fingering the strands of his hair, pulling him even closer to me, because it's still not enough, I need more.

He must sense my frustration because he lifts his mouth from me and begins unbuttoning his slacks, pulling his cock free. He's so hard The thick head of his cock is red and angry, after being denied for so long. Hooking his arms around my hips, he hauls me down to the end of the exam table and drives inside me in one thrust, and it has us both gasping at the connection.

In this position, he's so deep, and I feel so full that my head swims. Sex has never felt like this. So good. So perfect. I've never felt so in tune with another person than I do whenever I'm with him.

"You feel so fucking good." He grunts, thrusting hard. The sound of our filthy fucking fills the exam room, echoing off the walls. His rough, ragged breaths, my pleas for more, the sound of skin slapping together in rhythm as he rocks into me.

I feel my orgasm building; I can almost grasp it, but it's still just out of reach. Tonight's foreplay has my body tight with tension, and I can feel myself barreling toward the edge, ready to fall completely.

Parker slows his thrusts, glancing down between us, watching his cock as it fills me. He uses his thumbs to open me wider, and he hisses when I tighten around him, his eyes darting up to meet mine. He slams back inside me, so deep and so hard that my toes curl on the sides his hips.

"Come for me, love," he commands, dropping his finger to my clit. The contact is all it takes for my orgasm to unfold, my body tightening with release.

"Parker." I moan, writhing on the table as he continues fucking me through my orgasm. I buck against his fingers, the pleasure too much for my throbbing, sensitive clit.

"Good girl, just like that. Soak my cock."

He plants himself deep, one hand holding my hip, the other traveling to my throat, where he grips lightly as he comes. I can feel him tremble as he rides it out with small, shallow thrusts as he empties inside me. I'm flooded with his cum, and it's a feeling that I'm quickly becoming addicted to.

Once we've come down from the bliss of our orgasms, I grip his chin and smirk. "If this is how you treat all of your patients, no wonder you're the most popular doctor in town, Dr. Grant."

"I'm the *only* doctor in town, Quinn."

Semantics.

Chapter Seven
QUINN

"HAR HAR"
— QUINN SCOTT

After the longer than anticipated stop at his office, not that I'm at all complaining, we go back to Parker's for the night. The moment the front door is opened, Marshmallow comes barreling toward us, attacking us with kisses and a bucket full of slobber.

"Hi, sweetie puff. I'm going to call you that from now on. Get it…Marshmallow…puff?" I'm talking in a high-pitch baby voice since, obviously, the dog is the sweetest baby on earth, and Parker just shakes his head and laughs as he shuts the front door.

He hangs our coats on the rack, still wet from the snowfall, and walks into the kitchen, calling back over his broad shoulder, "I've got big plans for you, Quinn Scott."

"Oh? And what do these plans consist of?" My voice

is laced with arousal. I can't help it; the man makes me addicted to him.

"Dirty girl. We're going to make cookies." He smirks, pulling out a cannister of flour and placing it on the counter. "You up for it, Scrooge?"

"Har, Har. Yes, I'm up for making cookies."

"When's the last time you made cookies?"

I shift on my feet, leaning over the granite island toward where he's arranging the ingredients and everything required to bake the cookies. "Uh, more like when's the last time I made anything? I honestly can't even remember the last time I cooked. My meals generally consist of takeout at the office, or a slice of pizza on the way home. Super healthy, I know."

Parker frowns before shaking his head. "I guess I can save my lecture on nutrition for later. You gotta take better care of yourself, love. You're going to work yourself to death before you're thirty."

I've heard this time and time again, from my mother, from Owen. Even from my friends.

"Yeah, well, I'm trying this new thing where I relax, so we'll see how things go. Plus, I'm up for a really big promotion at work, one that I've worked my ass off for, and once I get it, I won't have to spend as much time at work. The position comes with an assistant, and that will be freaking great."

Even though he has no idea what goes into my day, or what it is that I really do, he listens intently, and the look on his face shows that he actually cares.

"Is there anything that you can't do?" I tease. "You're a doctor, and a great one at that. You volunteer at the nursing home and are some kind of sex god. And you even bake cookies. You're the perfect man."

"Nah, no one's perfect, Quinn. Everyone has their faults, including me," he says.

I can't stop my eyes from rolling. "Says the perfect man. It feels strange sometimes. I feel like I know you so well. I mean, we grew up together. I know your favorite movie, and every time you've had stitches. Your favorite sports. How old you were when you lost your virginity. But then, sometimes I feel like I don't know you at all. The man you are now."

"Well, get to know me again, Quinn. I'm still the boy you knew, but now, I'm a man. We've both changed over the years."

For the hundredth time since I fell into his bed, I think

about the next few days and how after it's over, I'll be hundreds of miles away again, and my sleepy, small town will be in the rearview once more.

"I'm leaving, Parker. You know this."

He nods, an inquisitive expression on his face as he leans against the granite. The material of his dress shirt pulls around his arms.

"Why are you so ready to run?"

The question takes me by surprise, hitting me directly in the chest with so much force that I take a step back.

"I'm not running anywhere, Parker. New York is my home now. Not Strawberry Hollow. Not anymore. My life is there. My career, my friends, my apartment. Please, let's not ruin the small amount of time we have left together, worrying about things that we can't change. Let's bake these cookies, okay?"

For a moment, he only stares at me, his eyes stormy and dark, then he nods and walks over to the fridge and grabs a carton of eggs.

If we're going to enjoy the last bit of time we have, we've got to fall back into the comfortable banter between us.

"Hey, Alexa, play 'Rockin' Around the Christmas Tree,'"

I say softly, walking around the island and taking my spot next to him.

The Christmas classic, that even I can admit is catchy, floats through the speaker, and I can see Parker's lips flatten as he suppresses a smirk.

"Now, come show me what to do because it's been so long that I've forgotten. Where are the cutters?"

An hour later, we've got the dough rolled out and more flour on everything around us than on the actual cutting board.

"Okay, favorite Christmas movie. And don't say 'none.' You have to choose. Out of all the ones you've seen, what's the best?" Parker asks as he uses the tree-shaped cutter on the flattened dough. His strong hands flex with every movement, and god, I never realized how sexy hands could be, not until seeing Parker use his for a magnitude of things.

I pull my lip between my teeth as I think.

"And by favorite, you mean which do I hate the least?"

He laughs. "Yeah, that."

"What's yours?" My fingers carefully break free the sugar cookie dough around the cutter, leaving behind the perfect gingerbread man.

"Either...*Elf*, or *The Santa Clause* with Tim Allen."

I pretend to gag, sticking my finger down my throat. "Will Ferrell. I hate him. I don't know why, something about him just irks me. My least favorite actor of all time. *Especially* in anything Christmas-related."

"I can't believe you just said that," Parker says, his face covered in disbelief. "The man is literally on the Hollywood Walk of Fame, and you're going to disrespect him like that?"

"Oh God, what are you, head of the Will Ferrell fan club? He is not funny and is so cringe."

Parker opens his mouth, as if he's going to say something, but then shakes his head and closes it. I can see his jaw working.

The next thing I know, he's tossing flour at me, landing with a dusty poof along my cheek.

I'm too stunned to speak, or to even respond.

Parker Grant just threw flour at me. On my face.

Glancing down, I sputter when I see that it's now covering my vintage cashmere sweater.

This. Is. War.

I don't even say anything. I just take one of the closest things to me, which just so happens to be an egg, and I crack it right over the top of his smug head. The yolk runs down his hair onto his cheek, and the look on his face?

It's priceless.

One that I would pay to see over and over again.

It's rare to be able to render Parker speechless.

Grinning, I step back and cross my arms over my chest, not backing down in the least.

"Sure you wanna do this, love?"

He swipes at the runny egg that's sliding down his face and flings it onto the counter, his eyes darkening when they catch mine, and for a second, I regret said egg.

Only for a single second though.

His stare becomes predatory, and I turn on my heel and make a run for it. There's no way that I'm going willingly, if he wants me, he's going to have to catch me first.

I make it all of six steps before his arms snake around my waist, pulling me back against his hard body. His hands are full of icing, and he makes quick work of rubbing it all over my face until my vision is icing-filled, and it's caked everywhere.

"You can run, Little Scott, but I'm always going to catch you." His words are hot and delicious against my ear, and my body acts on his own accord, pressing back against him.

"You started it."

His fingers slip under the fabric at my stomach, then he bunches it into a fist and flips me around to where his lips hover over mine, only a breath away.

"And I'm going to finish it."

Later, when we're both naked and still covered in flour, tangled together on the kitchen floor, I find myself thinking about how easy it is to be with Parker. To forget everything else when I'm in his arms. It's effortless.

And that's exhilarating as much as it is terrifying.

My head rests on his chest while the other parts of my body are partially on top of his, partially on the cool tile of the kitchen. I couldn't even recall how long we've been here, only that we are both completely sated and laughing about stories from our past.

That's one of the things that makes this so easy. Parker has always been a permanent fixture in my life. He knows me almost better than I know myself at times.

Lazily, he drags his fingers along my spine as he holds me, in no hurry to move us from the spot on his kitchen floor.

"That wasn't exactly what I had in mind when I said I wanted us to bake cookies." He laughs. "But...I'm game for Christmas baking any time you want, love."

"Don't tempt me. I'm always down to see you get dirty, Dr. Grant. Did any of the cookies even survive?"

I ask, rising up slightly to peer over the island, even though I can't actually see anything because it's so high.

Parker laughs and his entire massive body rumbles beneath me, "Don't think so, but still, it was fun. Plus, I've gotten you to listen to Christmas music for four hours, and we even attempted to bake cookies together. I think I'm going to win this bet, Little Scott."

Leaning back, I narrow my eyes. "Not a chance in hell. It'll be the perfect sendoff present, seeing you prance around in bright green tights. I'm taking a video, so I can keep it forever."

Parker growls and rolls me over, covering my body with his, and suddenly, the bet and anything Christmas-related is nothing but a afterthought.

The next morning, I drag myself from Parker's arms in his warm, entirely too comfortable bed, and throw on a pair of leggings and a sweater before running a brush through my thoroughly fucked hair. Hopefully, my mother doesn't pay much attention when she gets home because even my lips look red and swollen from Parker's kisses.

"Ready?" he says, peeking his head around the door in the bathroom.

"No?"

Laughing, he leans in and presses a quick kiss to the top of my head before turning back toward the bedroom. Today he's wearing a Chicago Avalanches hoodie and a faded pair of blue jeans, and truth be told, I've hardly been able to keep my hands off of him.

How the man can look so delectable in literally anything he wears is beyond me.

Unlike me, I look like someone who lives under the interstate in most casual wear.

Entirely unfair, if you ask me.

"Let's go, Quinn," Parker calls from somewhere in the house. I can hear his keys jingle, and I groan out loud.

I quickly grab my overnight bag and join Parker in the living room.

"Let's get this over with."

He laughs, looping his arm around my neck and pressing his lips to my forehead. "It'll be fine. We'll just act normal."

"Yep."

Famous last words.

**

"Excited for tomorrow?" Owen asks, shoveling another piece of my mom's famous peanut butter balls into his mouth.

"I guess so. Things still feel kind of weird with Dad, but he's trying, so I feel like I have to too."

Owen nods. "It'll probably be like that for a while, sis."

He's right, but at least Dad is trying. We owe it to each other to at least try.

Mom sets another plate of Christmas treats down in front of us and my stomach growls. With as much sugar as I've had today, I'm going to have to run five miles at the gym every day when I get back home. There's no way that I can eat all of this and not gain five pounds.

If only my body didn't work this way. Sigh.

"Eat up, Quinn. Who knows when you'll be home next, so I can actually feed you. You're looking like skin and bones. All of that takeout you're eating is not sticking, sweetie," Mom says.

"Mom, please. The last thing on the planet I can be called is skin and bones."

I feel a nudge against my side and glance over to see Parker narrowing his eyes at me. He leans in, his lips barely brushing against the shell of my ear. "Next time I hear you talk badly about yourself, I'm going to put you over my knee and spank the fuck out of your ass."

Oh my God.

I can feel my face heat as a flush spreads from the top of my head down to my neck. He did not just say that with my brother, his best friend, across the damn room!

"Okay, what in the hell is going on?" Owen barks, his eyes darting between the two of us. "Are you...wait. Are you guys...banging?"

"Jesus Christ, Owen, don't say banging. You're not a teenager," Mom quips.

She walks over to the table and sits next to Parker, taking an iced sugar cookie off the platter,

"They're obviously engaging in sexual relations and you're making this very awkward for your sister."

This is the worst moment of my life. I'm fairly certain, at least. I wish the floor would actually open up and swallow me whole. Put me out of my misery. Please.

"Would you both stop," I screech, covering my face. "First of all, even if I was sleeping with someone, I don't need to discuss it with anyone, and definitely not over Christmas lunch! Second, there is nothing going on with Parker. We're friends, we've always been friends since we were kids."

"Actually, that's not true."

I whip my head to look at Parker, my jaw now hanging open. What in the hell is happening?

"Owen, I like your sister, and even though I'm pretty sure she's going to give me a black eye for saying it out loud, I'm going to pursue her, and I hope you'll be okay with it because it's not changing."

Groaning, I drop my head back as I mutter, "Parker!"

"What?" He shrugs, his shoulder dipping slightly in his old hoodie. "It's true, and hiding things never gets anyone anywhere."

I look up and see Owen's eyes oscillating between the two of us, his jaw hardened. He looks partially confused and partially pissed, and right now, I'm not sure which one I would rather him be.

"So, you're together?"

"No," I say.

"Kind of," Parker says.

I whirl toward him. "This is not a conversation that

we should be having at the table with my family, when it's certainly not one we've had in private."

The man has obviously lost his mind. In two days, I'll be on a plane headed back home.

Whatever is happening between us always had an expiration date, and I thought he knew that.

"So what, you've been just...having sex with each other the entire time you've been home? Really Quinn?"

Now I'm angry. I don't need Owen's condescending, judgmental tone, or him judging me in the first place. I'm not a teenager anymore and as much as I love and respect him, this is my life and I make my own decisions.

"Oh, shut it, Owen. If I want to have sex with Parker, I will, and there's nothing anyone can do about it. Sometimes you forget that I'm not sixteen anymore and I don't need you or anyone else telling me how to live my life." I stand from the chair abruptly, the wood scraping loudly against the floor. "Would it be so bad if Parker and I were together?"

"No," Owen sputters, "I just...I don't know, Quinn. He's my best friend, he's basically like family."

"There's nothing familial about how I feel about your sister," Parker adds.

Why do those words cause me to tingle the slightest bit? Because I'm obviously deranged, that's how.

"Look, I don't care if you and Quinn are together, okay? It just took me by surprise is all. I mean, we've just all been friends since we were kids, and I didn't expect this, I guess. I'm not mad. Quinn is right, it's her life."

"We're not together," I say again. Because as much as I appreciate him saying it, the fact remains that Parker and I are not together. "I need some air."

Before anyone can say another word, I turn on my heel and flee for the front door. Once I wrench it open and step outside, the cool air hitting my cheeks, I take my first full breath since I sat down.

I suck in gulp after gulp, trying to regain control of the situation that spiraled before I could stop it. Gradually, my racing heart slows, and I no longer feel like I'm suffocating.

God, what have I done?

Part of me knew not to get involved with Parker because of how messy things could become, and maybe I should've listened because this is a mess.

All of it.

My feelings for Parker, his feelings for me. The fact

that I live hundreds of miles away and he's here, in our hometown, with no plans to leave.

The fact that this was supposed to be a one-week fling with my brother's best friend, a forbidden, thrilling friends-with-benefits tryst that was going to be over before it really started.

At some point when I am lost in thought, the front door opens, and suddenly Parker's beside me, leaning over the front porch rail and gazing out into the darkness. At first, he doesn't say anything.

We both just stand side by side, neither of us knowing exactly what to say.

Finally, he speaks.

"I'm sorry that I said something back there when you weren't ready, and I'm sorry that I didn't say it to you privately first. But I'm not sorry for how I feel, Quinn."

My lower lip trembles slightly, hot, stinging tears welling in my eyes. Today has been full of so many emotions and I'm having a hard time processing it all.

"Love, look at me, please," he begs.

I drag my gaze to his and suck in a sharp breath when I see the sadness in his eyes. I will my own tears away, telling myself to get it together.

Easier said than done.

"This has become complicated, Parker, and I hate complicated," I say quietly.

Parker shakes his head then reaches for my hand. His fingers lace with mine, and for a second, I lean on his warmth. I always feel safe and cared for when I'm with him, which doesn't help the war raging between my heart and my head.

"Why does it have to be complicated? I know you feel how I do, Quinn. Hell, the same thing I've felt for years, only now, it's not something that I can ignore. It's not something that I'm just willing to let you walk away from," he whispers, turning my head toward him by grasping my chin. Our eyes lock. Steady. Intense. All-consuming. "The last week with you has been incredible, Quinn, and I know you feel the same. It feels natural as any relationship should. I'm not saying that it will be easy, and I don't even know how we would do it, I'm just asking you to try."

I pull my lip between my teeth and tear my gaze from his. This is crazy.

My life isn't here. It's in New York.

I find myself saying the only logical thought that flits through my mind. "You know this would never work."

His jaw clenches, the thought hardening his expression. "No, I don't know that. I just know that I'm standing outside in the fucking freezing cold, trying to convince a girl I'm crazy about that we're worth giving it a shot. Try with me, Quinn, and if it doesn't work, then we walk away, but at least we can say we gave it our all. We tried."

As badly as my heart wants to give in, wants me to throw myself into his arms, I know that life isn't so black and white, and things like this aren't easy.

A long-distance relationship takes hard work and patience. Time and dedication. All things I don't know for sure that I have because of my job.

"I need to think, Parker...my head is a mess, and I just need time to think things through, to weigh everything," I tell him.

Parker nods, his face a mask of hurt. "Meet me tomorrow, under the mistletoe. Just like we planned. Have your answer then, for this, for the bet, for everything. I'll be waiting, okay?"

"Okay," I whisper.

I can feel his lips at the top of my head as he presses them there gently, and then he's walking away, toward the old truck that I've ridden around in for half my life. The man that I've known for over half my life, but now see in a whole new way, driving it away.

Am I willing to take the risk and fall with him?

He makes it seem so easy, but there is more at stake here than a simple bet.

Chapter Eight
QUINN

HONESTLY, CHRISTMAS IS JUST ONE STRESSFUL
DAY A YEAR, WHERE PEOPLE COME
TOGETHER TO GIVE EACH OTHER GIFTS. I DON'T GET THE HYPE.

— QUINN SCOTT

I wish that I could say the answers come easily. But the truth is, I've spent the last twelve hours wallowing in the guest bedroom at my mother's house, stuffing my face with whatever Christmas cookies or desserts she brings me and pretending that the world isn't right outside these frosted windows.

"Are you going to wear that to your father's Christmas party, Quinn?" My mother asks as she slides another plate full of snacks onto the bedside table. Her brow is furrowed in worry, and judging by the level of hovering she's accomplished since everything happened, she is beyond the point of concern.

I glance down at the mumu I'm wearing of hers. It's got all nine reindeer (including Rudolph) and Santa riding up the shoulder and down the back. I cried a little putting it on, not just because it's the tackiest thing I've ever seen, but it feels like a new low for me, crying in a mumu in my mom's guest room.

"Of course I'm not going to wear it," I retort snarkily. Even though I have considered it and decided it was a strong possibility.

How ironic…me in a holiday-themed anything.

"Alright, it's time to get up, Quinn Scott. You are not going to lie in this room and wallow for another second." Mom comes over to the bed and sits on the edge, a look of compassion on her face. She leans forward and brushes my hair away from my face, and it brings me back to when I was a teenager.

The first time I ever had my heart shattered. I felt like the world was over, and the walls of death were closing in upon me, as most broken-hearted teenage girls would. Mom made all of my favorite foods and made sure that she was there to wipe away each and every tear. She even crawled in bed and ate ice cream with me.

This moment feels full circle. Here I am again with her by my side, comforting me like I'm still that broken-hearted, tear-stained teenager. Only now, I'm facing a decision I never imagined I'd have to make, one that might break my own heart.

"I know right now your heart is conflicted, baby girl, and I know that the right answer may not feel like the easy one, but no matter what you decide, I know that you'll navigate whatever life throws your way. You've always been resilient like that, Quinn. It's something I have always admired about you."

Fresh tears well in my eyes, and I sniffle, trying to keep them at bay.

"Just trust your gut. Even if it seems scary, and much bigger than you, trust your instincts. It won't steer you wrong. I know that true love is rare, and it's beautiful, baby. Sometimes it only comes around once in a lifetime and when you least expect it. I know better than anyone that you can't let past experiences make you bitter or make you fearful of the risk. You'll figure it out, and I have no doubt that you'll end up exactly where you belong."

Sniffling again, I reach out and pull her into my arms, letting my head rest on her shoulder as the tears fall freely now. "Thank you, Mom. For always knowing the perfect thing to say."

"A lifetime of learning, baby. Mistakes are always going

to happen, but if you follow your heart, it'll guide you home. Wherever that may be." Mom rubs my back as she talks, reassuring me.

She makes it seem a hell of a lot easier than what it feels like.

I flop back against the mattress, despite her trying to shoo me from the bed like a herd of cattle, and close my eyes, letting my thoughts wander.

A few moments later, the door opens, and my brother saunters through, shutting the door behind him. He flops down next to me on the bed, joining me.

"Don't let him go, Quinny," he says simply, as if he's weighing in on a casual conversation and not the trajectory of my entire life after tonight.

"Oh, are you giving life advice now, Owen?"

I feel his shoulder shrug next to mine. "If that's what it takes for you to pull your head out of your ass."

My elbow jabs him in the ribs, but not hard enough to knock him out of his spot next to me in the bed.

"Yesterday, you were outraged that we were together, and now you're team Parker?" My heart constricts at the mention of his name, and I hate that nothing will be the same after this week.

"I wasn't outraged. I was surprised and shocked. There's a difference. Look, I'm never going to be the one with sage advice, that's always been you. You've always been the one who could look a challenge in the eye and never once blink. You've always fearlessly followed your dreams and never hesitated to take what you want, Quinn. I have always been so fucking proud of you and how you grew up, even if I was, sometimes still am, overprotective. I was that way growing up because I wanted you to have the world, and the only thing I could offer that you didn't already have was to beat the shit out of anyone who hurt you."

A watery laugh escapes me because nothing could be more true. Owen would have punched any kid who looked at me sideways when we were kids.

"You've never been afraid of anything, and you can't start now. Parker is my best friend, and he's the best fucking guy I know. Without a doubt. And if he's what makes you happy, then that's all that matters to me. Both of you being happy. And I've seen the way that he looks at you, Quinn. He looks at you like you're the only person in a room full of people."

The tears flow heavily now. I'm unable to stop them as I cover my mouth and lean my head against Owen's shoulder.

"I can't give up my life in New York for a feeling, O. For something that's barely been happening for a week and is still unknown."

"I don't think he's asking you to. I think all he asked for was for you to figure it out together. If you wanna walk away, Quinn, and forget it ever happened, then I'll support you, but I think you're making a mistake if you do. Think about what it would be like to walk away and never look back. Think about what you'd be leaving behind. Are you really ready to do that?"

Could I leave Parker behind? For what? A job that I hate and have openly admitted to him that I hate? For a boss that makes me miserable every single second of my day? For a city that I love, and friends that I love…but where I feel alone more often than not?

I sit up abruptly. "I'll see you at the party, I've got to get ready. I think…I know what I need to do. Thanks for the advice, O. Love you. And thank you for always being my protector, even when I thought I didn't need it."

"Always, Quinny. Always."

When I walk into my dad's house hours later, the party is already well on its way. There's a man playing piano, the tune of "O Christmas Tree" floating through the air, and I see the incredible job Maria did with decorating. The entire house has been transformed into a winter wonderland that rivals the Waldorf's decor.

"Wow," I murmur, taking in the faux icicles that are as tall as me, along with the fake snow, the glittering white lights that wrap around the staircase banister and the snowy garland draped everywhere. There's a snowflake ice sculpture that towers over me as I make my way through the crowded ballroom.

I am *seriously* impressed and blown away. I was expecting a party, but this is unbelievable.

"Quinn! Hi! You're here."

Glancing over, I see Dad walking toward me with Maria at his side. She's wearing a long, silver gown that complements her pale, milky skin, and for a moment, I am envious that she is so effortlessly beautiful. Dad's wearing a gray suit that matches her shade of silver and a bright red bowtie.

"Hi," I smile, quickly hugging them both, "you two look incredible, and Maria, this party...you really outdid yourself. It's breathtaking."

Her cheeks pink, a flush hitting them at my compliment. "Oh, it's nothing. It's a special occasion, having everyone here together for the first time, so I wanted to be sure that everyone had a wonderful evening. I think I just saw your mom by the bar if you're looking for her."

Already at the bar. Smart woman.

"You look absolutely beautiful, sweetheart," Dad says with a smile that makes my heart ache, reminding me how glad I am that we're putting things behind us and rebuilding our relationship. I've missed him. More than I was ever willing to admit. This trip changed that.

"Thank you."

My dress for tonight is one of my favorite gowns, a fancy one that I don't get the opportunity to wear very often. It's a dark emerald green in the softest silk you've ever felt that pools to the floor at my feet. The sleeves are long and fitted, giving it an elegant silhouette. The chest is

194

a sweetheart neckline. But the best part?

I'm currently wearing my red converse underneath it. As much as I love and cherish my Louboutins, we were not repeating the first night I was here. And the dress perfectly conceals my rebellious, but comfortable, footwear of choice.

"Well, we've got to go make the rounds and greet everyone. You know how hosting goes. But enjoy the party, darling, and we'll catch up in a bit," Maria says, pulling me back in for a quick hug. Dad follows with a lingering and meaningful hug of his own.

Once they've glided away, I stand in the middle of the ballroom alone, my eyes scanning over both familiar and unfamiliar faces, all in search of the one very familiar face I want.

There's only one real reason I'm here tonight, wearing a dress that makes me feel as beautiful as I've ever been, with my nerves causing my stomach to knot and my heart to skip beats.

Finally, I spot him. Exactly where he promised he would be, waiting under the mistletoe with a hopeful but nervous expression on his too handsome face. His hands are shoved into the pockets of his slacks as he looks around, but he hasn't noticed me yet. Just like a magnet, I'm drawn to him. I feel like I could find him no matter the size of the crowd, my eyes would find him on any busy street because of the pull between us.

I use this quiet moment to drink him in. The black shirt he's wearing is covered in candy canes, and I can't help the giggle that tumbles from my lips.

The man and his ridiculous Christmas spirit.

His jaw is tight, and his shoulders tense. I can feel his apprehension, even from my spot across the room, and I want to take all that nervousness away. I hate that I'm the reason that it's there in the first place. When his eyes finally drift to mine, time stops around us. The chatter, the music, the clink of glasses…all disappear.

All I see is him.

I make my way through the crowd, my eyes never leaving his until I'm standing in front of him. My hands are shaking as I twist them anxiously. I don't know why I'm suddenly so nervous.

Maybe because, after tonight, everything will change. Maybe because, I'm worried he's changed his mind.

"You came," he says quietly, his voice a hoarse whisper.

"It was never a question, Parker. My head just had to catch up with my heart." Stepping in, I lift my hands to his chest, desperate to touch him. I can't last another second without the connection. "Here we are, under the mistletoe. Just like we said."

We both glance up to the leafy-green mistletoe, adorned with bright red berries, that's hanging above our heads. The silly thing that started all of this, and the silly thing that right now I couldn't be any more thankful for.

Without it, would any of this have even happened?

It seems so silly to say that a Christmas tradition changed the trajectory of my trip home, changed my whole life, but it's true. And here we stand.

Back underneath it like the first night, only now, everything is different between us.

Parker's eyes hold mine as he slides his arms around my waist, anchoring me in place.

"And what's your answer, Quinn Scott? Is there still all of that Christmas disgust in your heart or have I changed your mind? Did I win the bet?"

Swallowing, I tamper down the emotion that rises in my throat, making it difficult to breathe. I concentrate on the now-familiar feel of his hands along the small of my back, and the way that his chest rises and falls as he awaits my answer.

Grounding myself in the safety of his arms. Pushing my hesitation and fear away. It has no place here. Not with us.

"Well…I'm not sure if I like Christmas again.…or if I just realized I like Christmas with *you*, Parker Grant."

His lips tug into a blinding smile. "I told you that I'd win, you know. I knew that somewhere in there was the girl that I knew. She's just now part of the woman I now know."

"I think she's been here all along. I just was so focused on building my career and this new life in New York, that somehow along the way I lost sight of what mattered. I pushed that girl aside."

"I like you just the way you are, Quinn. ALL of you. Even the grumpy Christmas version of you. Whatever way I can have you. That's the way I want you. I love your confidence and your drive. I love that you're fearless and ambitious. I love your attitude, your sass, your heart, and how kind you are. Whatever version you are or want to be, that's who I want."

My heart beats wildly in my chest at his words. I can't believe that we're standing here right now, that what was supposed to be a quick trip home has resulted in something so much bigger.

"Then, I'm yours. I don't know how we'll make it work with me in New York, but…"

"We'll do whatever it takes. There are planes, trains, and automobiles…and FaceTime. We can meet in the middle. We'll figure it out. We can figure out anything together." I laugh and the tears that welled in the corner of my eyes now wet my cheeks. He reaches out, swiping away a tear gently. "I just know that I want this, Quinn. I want you, and I'm not letting you get on that plane without being mine. Be mine. Fuck, just, I need you to be mine."

There's no hesitation. There's no doubt or question. It was silly to even think that there was. I've been his before I even realized it. Before either of us did. Perhaps I always have been. I guess a subconscious part of me knew that we'd end up here. Together.

I slide my hands around his neck and tangle my fingers in his hair, pulling him down to my mouth before whispering, "I'm all yours, Dr. Grant. Now take me home, and let's spend our last night together in a way we'll never forget."

His eyes dilate, flashing with lust, before he lowers his lips to mine and takes my mouth in a fierce kiss right under the mistletoe like a cliché Christmas romance movie.

Maybe Christmas isn't so bad after all. In fact, I might even be inclined to say that it's my least hated holiday. As long as I get to spend it with him.

I'm a *reformed* Grinch.

And I have Parker to thank for that.

Oh, and of course, the mistletoe, that ungodly pair of bright green tights, and a bet that I was *always* destined to lose.

The End

Epilogue
QUINN

"I'M A REFORMED GRINCH."
— QUINN SCOTT

❝Is that everything? Quinn…are you sure? I thought I saw
    something in your bedroom and I-"

    "Mom," I cut her off with a laugh, "that's
everything. We've checked twice. Now, take a deep breath
and try to relax, okay?" I bring my hands to her tense
shoulders and give her a reassuring squeeze. I know she's
as anxious as I am, but we've got this under control.

    I've been looking forward to today for so long that
I refuse to let anything stand in the way, including my
mother's helicopter hovering.

    "Okay, you're right. I'll see you outside. Give you a
chance to say goodbye."

    "Yeah, thanks, Mom."

    Once the front door closes behind her with finality,
I look around the small apartment that I've called home

for the past few years. These walls that have seen my good days and bad ones. The place where I found myself and allowed myself to grow into the person I am today.

Part of me is immensely sad to leave behind this apartment, and my life here in New York, but an even bigger part of me is looking so forward to the future that I can't stop to look behind me.

"Ready?" A deep rasp vibrates against my ear as a pair of strong, muscular arms slide around my waist and haul me back against a hard, warm body.

The voice of the man who stole my heart when I never expected it. The man who swooped back into my life and changed every single second of it after he did. The man who has made the last year of my life, the happiest it's ever been.

I turn in his arms with a deliriously happy smile on my lips. "As ready as I'll ever be, Dr. Grant."

He smirks at the use of my favorite nickname for him and pulls me tighter against his chest. I sigh with contentment and lay my head upon his chest, listening to the steady strum of his heart beating beneath his skin.

A year ago, I put everything I had into a relationship I wasn't sure would even survive the week, let alone hundreds of miles and months between us.

But it did. We made it. Long distance was nothing when we knew we had each other at the finish line.

Parker Grant is mine, and I am never letting him go.

"U-Haul is ready to go. I've got everything packed in tight, and your mom is ready to head to the airport," he says.

My eyes scan the empty apartment once more, and I know without a doubt, I'm ready. Even though a piece of me will always miss New York, I'm ready to go.

"Then it looks like we're ready," I tell him, rising on the tips of my toes to press my lips to his. His lips move over mine, his kisses turning hungry.

Growling against my lips, he says, "If you're mother wasn't in the car, I'd lay you down right here, so we could give your apartment a proper goodbye. After all, we've spent the last year christening every surface in here as often as we could."

God, did we.

When we decided to try long distance, neither of us knew how to make it work, or what we were going to do until we could be together again. All we knew is that we wanted to be together and that nothing was going to stand in our way.

So, whenever Parker could get away, he came to me. Sometimes on a red-eye in the early morning hours, where we had less than twenty-four hours to spend together. But we cherished those moments together, however short or long they were.

We made the most of it. And when he couldn't come to me, I went to him. I visited home every chance that I got. Not only for Parker, although he was the main reason, but to repair my relationship with my father and to spend more time with my mom and Owen.

Falling in love with Parker is the best thing that's ever happened to me. And it helped bring my family together in ways that I never imagined.

"There will be plenty of time for that when we get home."

"Home. *Fuck*, I love hearing you say that," he mutters, pressing his lips against my jaw, peppering small kisses along the expanse of it. "Say it again."

"I can't wait to go *home* with you, Parker Grant."

After an entire year, we're finally moving in together. Or more like I'm moving into Parker's house, and even though it's a little scary, it feels more right than New York ever has. Anywhere that Parker is...feels right.

His lips leave mine for the briefest moment. "Oh. Can't forget this."

Reaching behind him, he pulls something out of his back pocket, and holds it up between us.

I glance down, and groan when I see the photo held between his fingers.

"You promised."

"I did. But... I couldn't let this very important piece of history just get thrown out, love. How would I tease you about it with our kids one day?"

My stomach flips at the mention of children. It's not the first time he's said it, and each time, I find myself wanting a future full of them with Parker. Something I never really wanted before.

I look at the picture in his hands once more, remembering that day like it was only yesterday. The smiles on our faces, the way Parker's gazing down at me with adoration. The only thing to dislike about the photo is what I'm wearing in it. I *did* in fact wear those ungodly green tights and star in the Christmas production my mother put on.

And even though I lost the bet, I won the guy.

That's all that matters. At least, I think so.

"I still can't believe you looked this good in green tights." I smirk, dragging my gaze back up his. Thank God this picture exists, just in case I ever forget what his ass looked like in those tights.

He laughs, "And I still can't believe you somehow convinced me to do the damn play with you."

"Hey, I'm pretty sure that I made up for it after the fact. Several times in fact."

I pluck the photo from his hands and tuck it safely into the back pocket of my jeans then loop my arms around his neck.

Sometimes it's hard to believe that this selfless, kind, ridiculously handsome man is mine. That a bet turned into this.

That I've been lucky enough to love him for the past year.

Now, I'm headed back to Strawberry Hollow, and not just for Christmas.

For good.

Because it turns out that home isn't a place, it's wherever Parker Grant is.

Loved The Mistletoe Bet?

Here's a sneak peek at Jingle Wars!

ABOUT THE BOOK

From bestselling authors Maren Moore & Veronica Eden comes an all-new steamy new adult enemies-to-lovers holiday romcom standalone.

Two inns, one town, and there's not enough room for the both of them.

Add in a reindeer-ish donkey, a Christmas competition, and a rivalry to end all rivalries and you're bound to end up in disaster, right?

Finn Mayberry has enough on his plate trying to keep his Grandparents inn afloat. The last thing he needed was some California state of mind starlet bulldozing into his town and throwing up a five-star resort right next to his family's inn.

But, now she's here and he can't get her out of his town or his head.

Freya Anderson took one look at the snowcapped mountains of Hollyridge and fell in love. She's finally here and ready to take on the task of proving to her father that she can handle running Alpine.

She never expected to make enemies with the sinfully delicious lumberjack of a man who runs the inn next door. He's moody, impossible and completely off limits.

There can only be one winner, but you know what they say. All is fair in love and... Jingle Wars?

CHAPTER ONE
FINN

"Grams, seriously, there's nothing up here." Once again, my eyes search the dim, musty smelling attic for the specific decoration that she's asking for. There's practically everything else you can imagine, but no donkey riding a snowmobile. I've been up here for at least thirty minutes and each time I tell her it's not here she just hollers at me to look harder, because I'm missing it.

Right… Because donkeys riding a damn snowmobile are easy to miss.

"Oh Finn, shucks, just move some stuff around. I know your Gramps put it up there somewhere," she calls up to me.

I hear her muttering under her breath. As much as I love this woman, my patience is wearing about as thin as this reindeer sweater that she insisted we wear while we begin decorating for the Christmas season. One thing I've learned is that you don't tell Grams no. Well, unless you want to be eating sandwiches for a week. Wicked woman, bribing us with food.

"Are you sure Gramps put it up here? Remember last time when you swore that Gramps was the one to misplace the extension cord? Except you forgot you lent it to the bingo hall for their light display?"

I close my eyes, grab the bridge of my nose, and let out a disgruntled sigh.

"Don't sass me, Finn Michael!" she exclaims. I can hear the feigned exasperation in her voice from up here.

Christ.

Even though I know it's not here, I move a few more miscellaneous boxes around and look through them quickly. In the dim light, I can't make out much and I'm using my hands to feel my way through the attic. Of course, I catch my big toe on a wooden beam and the pain radiates up my leg.

"Shit! Ah, damn it!" I curse, grabbing my throbbing foot.

"Finn Michael Mayberry!" Grams calls up the ladder, chastising me.

Jesus, get me down from this damn attic.

My final sweep of the attic reveals no donkeys and

definitely not one riding a snowmobile, so I head back down the rickety ladder extended from the attic. The old wood creaks and groans under my weight and I make a mental note to add it to the never-ending list of things around here to fix.

Every time the wind blows, something else breaks or is on the verge of breaking, and there's not enough time nor money to go around.

"Finn, you in here?" My Gramps calls out from the living room. He's been working in the front all morning fixing and arranging everything exactly to Grams' liking until she came in here and put me on the mission of finding the damn donkey.

"In here, Harold!" she yells from her chair in the corner, where she's knitting yet another Christmas sweater of some sort.

"Finn, my boy, thank you for all of your help. You know how much your Grams and I appreciate you," Gramps says as he walks through the hallway door. Snow covers his shoulders and sits in the hair of his white beard. His red, wind- whipped cheeks make him look like a jolly version of everyone's favorite fat man. He's sporting one of Grams' newest creations, a sweater of a Christmas tree with actual fuzzy pom poms knitted into it. He's been grumbling all morning because they keep getting caught on everything. As much as he complains, he'd wear it regardless because he'd do anything for Grams. He walks over and claps me on the back, giving me a warm smile.

It's November first and that means the start of the Christmas season here at Mayberry Inn. Grams and Gramps have owned this inn since they were younger than I am now. I've lived in Hollyridge my entire life, and the Mayberry is where I grew up. I ran down these hallways with toys, and played with the guests' children on the front lawn having snowball wars until we were frozen solid from the cold.

Every memory from my childhood has a piece of this place, so I guess it's only right that it's my turn to take some of the reins, literally and figuratively. My grandparents are getting older and with Gramps' heart problems in addition to the scare that we recently had with said heart problems, they're forced to take a step back and not work so hard.

And that's where I come in. Now the place I once called home growing up is where I find myself once more. When they called, I packed up my small one-bedroom apartment and moved back in. Now, this will be my first year as the person running the inn. I'm determined to make Grams and Gramps proud and to make sure that this place is around for a lot longer. I've been using any free time that I have to do repairs. Paint, fix holes, work on the plumbing. I'm the first to rise and the last to lay my head down at night, but it'll pay off.

"It's nothing Gramps. We'll have this place fixed up in no time. I just wish you would've asked for my help earlier."

"Well, I tried to do it all myself, but you know this old ticker isn't allowing me to do much of anything anymore. With your Grams here on my back, I need to follow the doctors order and let my body rest," he says, his face falling ever so slightly. My heart squeezes at Gramps crestfallen face. I hate seeing him feel like this.

When you've put your heart and soul in something for the last fifty years, only to be told that your body won't allow you to anymore... It's a tough thing to wrap your head around. That's why I want to be here to help them as much as I can. It's up to me to restore the inn to its original glory.

"Don't worry Gramps." I give him a reassuring smile.

Grams looks up over the rim of her thin, gold metal framed glasses and says, "You know, Finn, me and the ladies at Pokeno last week were just talking about you."

And here we go...

"Mary Ellen has a granddaughter that is coming to visit for the holidays. I think it would be so lovely if you took her out and showed her the town."

"Christ. Grams, I do not need you setting me up with your friends' grandchildren. I am perfectly capable of finding a woman."

She grins ever so slightly. "I know that Finn, but you're creepin' in on thirty. You know that they consider women geriatric when they have children over thirty?" She huffs. "All the women in the town fawn all over you, why don't you just pick one already?"

Why am I single at twenty-seven? Because there's not a woman in this town that interests me enough to keep her around longer than the night. I wouldn't call myself a player or anything of the sort because my grandparents taught me to respect a woman. But I'm up front. They know exactly what they're in for from the start. I'm not looking for anything serious. The Mayberry is what has my full attention and I don't have time for any distractions.

"C'mon Grams. You know you're the only woman in my life." I grin.

Grams loves me, I know it, but the meddling drives me insane

She rolls her eyes and huffs, "Would you please do it, Finn? For me?"

This guilt trip is taking a turn for the worse, quickly. The look on her face is one that makes me feel bad and I haven't even done anything wrong. Dammit Grams.

"Fine. But it's not a date," I mutter.

Her face lights up and she hastily puts her knitting on the table beside her, then stands.

"Oh, I have to go call Mary Ellen and tell her! She will be so excited." She squeals then leaves me and Gramps standing there, off to gossip with her friends.

Gramps looks at me and laughs, clapping me on the shoulder once more. "Welcome to the past fifty years of my life, son. You do a lot of things you don't want to do for the women that you love."

Tell me about it.

* * *

It's late by the time we get all of the decorations unboxed and Saint Nick, the inn's resident mascot and reindeer/donkey has been tended to. With the house silent and still, I sit down in front of the crackling fire, thankful for the quiet moments that are rare in a house filled with people at all times. It's been an adjustment from having my own peaceful solitude to the hustle and bustle of guests. Even though bookings through what is usually the Mayberry's prime tourist season have been…light. Which worries me more than anything. Usually the inn is completely booked, no vacancies. That was my first sign that something wasn't right.

One thing that my grandparents have always believed in is family. The Mayberry may not be the biggest, or the fanciest inn in Hollyridge. It may have a few loose floorboards, and need a new coat of paint, but it's always been a place where guests can come to feel welcomed. Since the Mayberry's foundation is built on tradition, people enjoy coming here to spend quality time with their families. Each year we get a wave of the same familiar faces as families make visiting their own personal tradition.

But for the past few years…business has slowed down.

Greatly.

Kids get older, they get iPads, Instagram and TikTok, or whatever the hell they call it, and then spending face to face quality time with their families isn't very high on their list of priorities and yeah, I get it. Today's generation is much different than the one I was raised in. But that's what we're trying so hard to do here, preserve a place that is filled with love, tradition, and the real Christmas spirit. One that doesn't include TikTok.

Although it's hard to stay positive and cheery when the bills I see Gramps carry in every day weigh heavily on us all. We have three months and then the bank is going to foreclose on the property and everything that Grams and Gramps worked so hard to build. So, it's up to me to save the inn and make a legacy that our family can be proud of. No pressure, right?

About Maren

Top 20 Amazon Bestselling author, Maren Moore writes romantic sports comedies with hot as puck, alpha daddies. Her heroines are best friend material, and you can always expect a HEA with **lots** of spice. When she isn't in front of her computer writing you can find her curled up with her kindle, binge watching Netflix, or chasing after her little ones.

Get my Newsletter for Updates, sales and exclusive content: https://geni.us/NLMaren

Also by Maren Moore

Standalone
The Enemy Trap
The Newspaper Nanny

Totally Pucked Series
Change on the Fly
Sincerely, The Puck Bunny
The Scorecard
The Final Score

Coming Soon
The Ex Equation

THE MISTLETOE BET

Printed in Great Britain
by Amazon

34219407R00130